The characters and events portrayed in this book are fictitious. Any similarity to real persons, living or dead, is coincidental and not intended by the author.

For my brilliant, vibrant, inspiring daughter S. No matter what storms pass your way, may you always sail toward your dreams.

Chapter One

The storm raged recklessly off the coast of Malta. Verity had never been terribly seasick during previous travels with her father, but this time, she was huddled in a corner of her cabin, clutching a bin in the event that her usually iron stomach did not serve her well. The steamer was meant to take a full two weeks to reach Alexandria from Lisbon (to which they had traveled by train via Paris from London), but this sea swell had pushed them far from their original schedule – a prediction debated at length by her father with the captain of the ship.

Captain Bardot seemed to possess a great interest in her father. A well-renowned historian and anthropologist, Professor Columbus Easton could speak, albeit absentmindedly transitioning from one subject to the next, on a variety of intriguing topics. In turn, having never before encountered an American ship's captain, Professor Easton held the fearless leader of the mighty vessel in equal esteem.

Verity, but a girl of thirteen, would sit in the captain's quarters of an evening. Her back as straight as a sunflower reaching to its zenith, she would endeavor with all her might to suppress each yawn, even though the conversations between the two men would often stretch until dawn slithered her tawny tendrils over the luminous brass portholes.

Ever an attentive daughter, Verity would ensure her father's safe return to his cabin at the end of these conversations, tucking him in with an old plaid blanket that was thick with the scent of must. She had hidden it away when they were packing in hopes that he would forget it, but the professor had ferreted it out and insisted they take it, no matter how many times Verity assured him that they did, in actual fact, have blankets aplenty in Egypt.

It was these severe blind spots in the professor's logic that compelled Verity to care for him so very cautiously. His mind rested on other – to him, at least – more "essential" knowledge. Archaic discoveries and cultures of peoples long dead were the centers of his narrow universe. In fact, in these long discussions with Captain Bardot, he would often inquire about ancient American objects or traditions he had heard of or seen in his precious British Museum. Regrettably for the professor, the captain was a modern man with no interest in the history of his own country, aside from it giving him occasional berth from his beloved sea.

When the captain would hint at his lack of interest in these particular subjects, the professor would merely blink his mild eyes rapidly, at a complete loss as to why the man before him would not have delved intensely into the roots of the nation from whence he came. At these times, the professor's respect for the captain became moderately shaken. However, aside from a look that only Verity knew the truth of, the professor did not let on.

Rather than turn the exchange to a more fascinating subject for both men, he would obstinately expound an exponential amount of knowledge upon his friend, oblivious to the obvious boredom of the other.

It was only Verity who recognized the professor's disappointment, so reliable was her daughterly observance. She would occasionally slip in a word or two, redirecting the debate toward such subjects as she knew would please and delight both parties – a talent that her father never praised her for. Nor did he, in fact, take notice.

The captain, marginally more attuned to the intelligent attentions of the daughter, often looked at her with a twinkle of bemused gratitude in his eye.

Such an occurrence had happened earlier that evening. The professor was notably disappointed when the captain declined his invitation to a meal and a chat. The young but experienced seaman announced that a gale was brewing and that his crew was in need of his leadership. Ever the scholar, the professor could not fathom why the captain would give over an evening of stimulating conversation for "a bit of wind and rain." No such weather had ever prevented *him* from the pleasure of work or study.

"This is utter nonsense! Utter nonsense, I tell you!"

bewailed the man.

"I assure you, I am disappointed as well, Professor Easton. I would much rather spend an evening with you than face this infernal tempest."

"Well, what's keeping you, then? There seem to be dozens of sailors who know perfectly well what they're doing. I'm always tripping over them one way or another. Can't they do without you for just one evening?"

"I'm afraid not, sir," replied Captain Bardot.

"Damn, hell, and blast it!" cried the petulant professor.

It was at this moment that the captain's eyes appealed to Verity's.

Clueing in quickly, she ameliorated, "Come along, Professor. I'm certain we can find something amusing to do."

For Verity never called him "Father" or "Papa" as other girls were wont to do. It was always "Professor," and it suited them both quite well. At times, she was teased for it at school, but she shook each insult off as raindrops from an umbrella. It really was of no consequence what the other girls thought. Invariably surrounded by clever and fascinating adults that passed through her home, she never curried the favor of her peers. Rather, she stood in awe of the best minds of the day who could discourse far more fascinating subjects than she ever overheard in the schoolyard.

Occasionally, she wondered if there was a time before, when her mother was still alive, that she had called the professor by any affectionate terms. Had she ever been a lisping child of two or three, calling out to her "Papa?" If such a season ever had existed, the memory was long extinguished, and she did not yearn for it.

As her thoughts lingered upon the past, she found herself neglecting her duties in the present. Instead of discovering an alternate activity, as she had assured the captain, she instead ensured the professor's safe return to his cabin, a habit that she often undertook. In the absence of her mother and the absent-mindedness of the professor, she felt a great responsibility toward him.

Oftentimes, Verity would discover the professor curled up, asleep in odd corners of the house, and would be forced to incur his puerile wrath when she awakened him to encourage his retreat into his bedchamber. Once, on the ship, she had a knock on her cabin door to discover a sailor who complained that he couldn't access his private store of whiskey as the professor had fallen asleep draped over a barrel. How he could have made his way to that odd corner of the ship, she never discovered, but she was careful to ensure that he was safely tucked away in his own cabin every evening after that for the duration of their journey.

As the steamer began her dance with Poseidon, the passion between the two was fraught with rage. Spasms of vehemence played out between them until Verity's strength was nearly wasted. Twice she looked in on her father, gladly observing that he rested peacefully in his cabin. A third attempt proved to be a grave mistake. The wrath of the sea made its mark upon her equilibrium, and by the time she returned to her own quarters, a paroxysm of nausea washed over her.

Retching over a bin, she nearly fainted with the effort. Boiled halibut had never been her favorite, but combined with giblet soup and hollandaise sauce…

Verity could not recall feeling so utterly miserable. When it was all over, she placed her head fastidiously in the center of her cool feather pillow and covered herself all the way up to her neck with the comforting duvet, shrouding herself in a veritable cloud of comfort.

As soon as sleep overtook her, the dream began.

It often commenced in the same way. She could feel something cold enclosed in her grasp – metallic and glittering, although she never knew what it was. Whilst awake, she often thought it could be a string of jewels or a bracelet. Constantly aware of the feel of it in her hand, this was the primary sensation she carried along with her from dream to dream.

The next pleasure she felt was the sun. Not the shimmering, dappled light of the English days she knew, but the hardened, sultry heat of a land unknown. Dry and piercing, she relished the feeling as it tingled upon her skin.

The whispering of palm trees above her always ensued. As she walked forward, she could feel their momentary shade lick at her arms, and she shuddered a little. It was the daylight she worshiped – longing to have its heated rays meld into her until it was part of her inmost being.

An almost-imperceptible noise would draw her attention from the dancing fronds and sultry brilliance above her. She would turn to see what it was, and…from this point on, the slumbering fantasy could never be remembered in her waking hours. She always knew that she walked and laughed and tasted and touched, but where, at what, or with whom, she never could recall.

It was always the same dream...the same beginning, and Verity let out a breathy sigh of contentment as the familiar, enchanting world washed over her.

Chapter Two

Verity's dark, bobbed hair blew about in the breeze as she leaned over the railings on deck near the prow. Although the night she'd spent had begun miserably, her half-remembered dream and the morning sea seemed to make up for it, respectively, with delicious memories and sparkling, smooth waters. The sun was bright, but she could not feel its warm breath upon her cheek, for the wind – always a companion to the ocean – was out in full force. She gave in to its wildness lustily, removing a smart little cloche hat as she did so. The professor had purchased it for her during a fit of generosity, and she was loath to lose it to a passing whirlwind.

She laughed at the white-cheeked terns whose calls lent a thrilling atmosphere to the scene – their feathers cutting in sharp angles across the sky. As the ship chased the horizon, she followed the sun's rays, darting across the blue, until she bent far over the railings to see them kiss the bottom of the ship. Was that a sea turtle she could see hurrying in its lumbering fashion as fast as it could away from the shadow of the boat? Verity sighed as she straightened up. How could she be unforgiving of last night's miseries when the ocean gave so generously to her on this fine morning?

"You seem to be enjoying yourself, young lady," said a rich voice behind her.

With all of the tender awkwardness of youth, Verity plunged her cloche upon her head, tucking away her hair behind her ears as she turned around.

"It is a very nice day, indeed," she responded faintly, observing a finely dressed man in a well-cut overcoat, buttoned to the chin.

"I didn't mean to startle you. You have my apologies."

He tipped his hat, then pulled it down more closely about his ears. Verity's eyes danced with mischievous merriment. Youth always seems to carry an inexplicable wealth of bemusement and contempt for anyone older than themselves. In this case, although the man could not have been much above thirty-five, Verity viewed his attempts to protect himself against the mild elements as positively ancient.

Catching her look, he joined in her silent mirth as he smiled and said, "Yes, I confess, even on a lovely day such as this, I still crave the warmth of my homeland. Thank Allah I shall be there soon."

Verity's expression immediately changed from artless glee to fascination.

"You are going home...to...to Egypt, then?"

“Yes, my child. I had business in Europe, but now I am coming back again.”

The man smiled to himself as he looked out over the ocean.

“You can almost make out the tip of the port of Alexandria – just there.”

He pointed southward, his hand nearly striking her face in the energy of his excitement. Verity did indeed see an infinitesimal row of buildings as they came within the scope of their vista. Inside of her stomach arose the slightest trickling of butterflies, not for the near miss of the stranger’s arm, but for sight of the place that would soon be her home as well.

The professor had been ambiguous about the details of his assignment from the British Museum. Always living in an ancient time within the confines of his own intellect, Verity found it problematic to catch precisely the purpose of his pursuit. But after abundant probing and a little research, she had ultimately ascertained the sum of what had transpired.

A red ochre fragment had come into the possession of the museum, and the professor and a few colleagues had fought over it, akin to a charm of hummingbirds battling over a particularly fragrant flower. When the rivalries settled, and it was determined that Professor Easton was the foremost authority on Egyptology, it was therefore handed over to his care in order to translate it.

The professor was not disappointed in his findings. The shard of stone intimated that the final resting place of Nefertiti was not, as previously suspected, near the tomb of her son, Tutankhamun, but considerably farther south, near Aswan. With this discovery, the museum gathered volumes of financial resources to ship the duo off to Egypt to see what could be discovered.

And so, with little preparation and great excitement, Verity's life was uprooted unceremoniously until she was transported here upon this ship, only miles from the land that she was peering toward expectantly.

Eyes straining to catch a more detailed glimpse of the prospect before her, Verity blinked rapidly as tears filled her eyes, rewetting them from the exsiccation of the wind. She sneezed, uncomfortably wiping her nose with the cuff of her coat, as she was neither old nor wise enough to remember to carry a handkerchief upon her person.

"What did you say?" queried the man sternly, as though the sternutation recalled him from a distasteful reverie.

As he saw the young girl wiping away at her sleeve, he proffered her a handkerchief apologetically.

"I've been terribly remiss in my manners, which I know you British value so highly. I am known as Sethos Chenzira Rashidi."

Giving a gentlemanly bow, he inquired, "And your name, young miss?"

"Verity Easton, daughter of Professor Columbus Easton."

A little shy of this stranger, Verity hoped the inclusion of her father in the introduction would increase his estimation of her.

"Well, Daughter of a Professor..." he annunciated the appellation as though it was a grand title. "What brings you to Egypt?"

Not waiting for an answer, he continued, "Or should I assume that your father will be probing the hidden depths of my country's history, along with a myriad of other so-called archeologists who have invaded our shores in the past few decades?"

His hand swept once again uncomfortably close to Verity as he gestured toward the land that was growing ever closer to them both.

Nodding thoughtfully, Verity was at a loss as to how to respond to his accurate, if acerbic, query.

Instead, she artlessly changed the subject and inquired, "Is it true that you're named for your father and grandfather?"

Mr. Rashidi's eye seemed to take on a new light as he more closely observed this young girl.

"Why, yes. It is tradition in my country. My father was Chenzira, my grandfather Rashidi. My family has kept with this custom, although it is quickly falling out of fashion. Many of my kindred have adopted a common surname, as you British do."

Verity did not quite understand why the man was saying the word "British" as if it was poison in his mouth.

"My mother was Egyptian," she inserted defensively, hoping this would somehow alleviate the tension that she could barely begin to fathom.

"Ah," said Mr. Rashidi, attempting to light a little white cigarette and giving up as the wind would not grant the flame of the handsome gold lighter life. "I thought there was something about you."

Much like the flame of the lighter, Verity was hungry for more illumination. She waited for Mr. Rashidi to explicate this observation, but she was disappointed. Abruptly, the man pulled up the collar of his overcoat high around his ears to meet his hat and walked away from her, around the prow, and to the other side of the ship, out of her sight.

Disturbed by this brusque departure with all the continued self-consciousness of her juvenility, Verity sought comfort in the beauty of the panorama before her. For, during her brief albeit frustrating conversation, the land seemed to have reached out to pull the boat toward it. The city of Alexandria, in all its splendor, was in sight, bright and golden in the morning's luminescence.

Chapter Three

Verity was considerably struck by the ivory-colored carriages of the train when they boarded in Alexandria. The crisp color, contrasting with the blackening of soot and dust, gave it the look of a child in short dresses who had been allowed to tumble about in the mud. It made Verity appreciate the thick, inky paint of the engine upon which no such tarnishment was noticeable.

Their compartment bounced to and fro as she fanned herself furiously with her rather ineffectual ostrich feather fan. They had been all the rage in England, and Verity insisted that it take a place of prominence in her meager travel case. It had served her very well in the occasional warmth of London, but this dry, oppressive heat was no match for the long, white, quickly thinning feathers. In fact, they seemed to wilt in defeat as she attempted to will them into the desired cooling effect.

Her poor father had succumbed in exhaustion to the

torridity and loosened his tie and collar – his suit jacket and vest acting as makeshift pillows against the window. A violent jerk of the train set his spectacles askew, and Verity reached to retrieve them, placing them carefully in their worn leather case.

Verity studied the professor's face. He was so innocent in many ways. Now, as he slept, he seemed a flushed little boy, unaware of the hardships that lay ahead of them both.

Looking back upon their journey thus far, the young girl wholeheartedly wished that they had been able to spend more time in Alexandria. The Library itself was enough to tempt her, but the professor had been eager to begin the expedition that he had been entrusted to complete. Despite many pleadings, they spent only one day in that fair city.

Now, they were bustling along in the train that would take them to Cairo, where they would stay only two nights. Next, they were to take a boat down the mighty Nile itself toward Luxor and the Valley of the Kings (which, indeed, the professor was interested in but planned to allow himself little time to enjoy), then on to Aswan near their final destination.

These thoughts encompassed Verity's mind as she considered what a radical shift one diminutive piece of stone could have upon both the course of perceived history and her own narrow life. She was arrested in her thoughts as the professor snorted forcibly in his sleep, the papers in his lap falling gently – almost peacefully – to the floor.

Verity gathered them together, pressing them flat as quietly as she could, and settled back into her seat. Often, she would read her father's notes out of boredom or curiosity. Riffling through the thick pages on her lap, she began to peruse the spidery scrawl of the professor:

Vengeance in Religion:
The Final Resting Place of Nefertiti: the
"Beautiful Woman Has Come"

Nefertiti and Akhenaten revolutionized the religion of their time by encouraging the axiom that the people of Egypt should worship a single god instead of many. Aten, the sun disc, was the focus of their fervor, and Pharaoh, along with his Great Royal Wife, became zealots in the passion of their beliefs. Many followed the rhetoric, because, during this religious transition, Egypt became wealthier than ever.

Some historians, myself included, believe that Nefertiti ruled after Akhenaten passed into the afterlife. However, when Nefertiti finally joined her husband in death, Tutankhamun, their son, became Pharaoh, and the country returned to worship the traditional gods.

Ever since Tutankhamun's tomb was discovered in 1922, my colleagues and I have devoted ourselves to studying where the final resting place of Tutankhamun's mother, Nefertiti, might be.

Many assume that she would have been buried in a tomb as splendid as her son's and possibly very near it. Others believe that Nefertiti and Akhenaten could have been buried together, as they passed to the underworld only seven years apart.

However, the remnant of the red ochre inscription that has come into my possession points to Tutankhamun's savage dismissal of his mother and her beliefs.

It hints that Nefertiti's theological fervency was distasteful to her son. Tutankhamun's wrath was unleashed upon his parents and their attempt to overthrow the ancient, polytheistic beliefs of his people. Within the inscription, he denounces them and commands that his mother's remains be banished southward, near modern-day Aswan, more than 140 miles down the Nile.

As only a scrap of the stone has been recovered, we are not certain of the location, but it does mention a temple devoted to the goddess Isis. One such temple, built much later than Tutankhamun ruled, was once erected on the island of Philae.

Although sites of ancient worship were often built on top of one another as wars, Pharaohs, and time passed, it is not my belief that Nefertiti's tomb is actually upon the island but much nearer Aswan. I have been in deep consultation with my colleagues, and there is enough evidence in other texts to lead me to believe that this temple of Isis mentioned is but a landmark for directional purposes.

As Verity was reading, a woman erupted into the train compartment. Smelling of the food recently served in the dining car, along with a little more sherry than she probably should have partaken of, the woman hiccuped violently as she settled herself directly across from her, maintaining an uncomfortably intense gaze as she did so.

"You don't mind if I jussst rest here for a moment, do you, dearie?" the woman slurred. "I cannot find my own com-

com-compartment, and I need to jussst steady myself for a moment. I get frightfully – hiccup! Frightfully sick upon these trainsss."

Verity nodded in shy assent, wrinkling her nose as the smell of liquor arrested her olfactories. Removing her intense stare, the woman hardly waited for Verity's tacit agreement before closing her eyes with a luxuriant moan.

The disruption of Verity's thoughts was, in fact, rather welcome, as her mind was teeming with ancient names, dates, and passions that weren't nearly so fascinating as the woman before her.

Swathed in layers of scarves and beads, the lady painted a stark and enthralling contrast to the individuals Verity was used to come in contact with. The professor's associates all wore nearly identical tweed suits, most of them with the addition of wire-rimmed spectacles, and they even seemed to share the same balding heads – their hair worn back by either nervous habits or genetics – Verity always wondered which.

Even Verity's own clothes were always plain and simply tailored, as befitted the child of a modest Professor. Therefore, this woman's unusual wardrobe was an absolute revelation to the young and impressionable girl.

After studying her closely, Verity observed that the lady's nails were painted – absolutely and thrillingly *painted* – a dark vermillion that she had only seen on the most flamboyant roses in Kew Gardens. Her dress was cut in the fashion of the day but married together with the most remarkable colors. Brilliant greens were stitched right alongside rich fuschias and saffrons, with fringe and tassels in abundance.

Verity audibly sighed as she stared enviously, but with no malice in her heart, at the woman's exotic wardrobe.

The unconscious exhale must have disturbed her unexpected guest, as one heavily blackened eyelash fluttered open and again locked gazes with Verity. The woman's icy blue irises seemed to penetrate into Verity's very soul.

Embarrassed, the girl attempted to break through her youthful awkwardness with, "I think your dress is very lovely."

Both cerulean eyes now widened with attentiveness.

Lamentably, the lady's speech continued in the slightly inebriated fashion in which it had begun: "Oh, d'you likesss it? I wasn't quite sssssure about the green, but a dear friend did talk me into it."

"Yes, it's very lovely."

"Thanksss you, my...my little dove," said the woman, who promptly fell asleep with her mouth agape.

Verity, satisfied with her effort at pleasantries, allowed the recherché woman to snore on. She even reached over and used Mr. Rashidi's handkerchief to wipe a trace of drool from the woman's mouth whenever necessary, preventing the saliva from ruining the dress Verity so admired.

Intermediately caring for the two unconscious individuals in her carriage, while not minding at all their chorus of snorts and wheezes, Verity enjoyed looking out the window, staring at the unusual and fascinating landscape. Long expanses of the amber desert stretched out before her. Rivulets made by the passing wind culminated in tiny, sandy peaks that made Verity imagine that such was the view of birds who soared high above the mountains.

As the train pulled at last into Cairo, Verity hastily tucked away the professor's papers, placing them neatly inside his carrying case. Gently, she awakened him with a little shake of the arm and handed him his glasses. Gingerly placing the kerchief in the lap of their unusual companion, she made a silent wish that their paths would cross again.

They deboarded the train as quickly as they could in the midst of the chaos that always accompanies such circumstances and were soon swallowed up by the madding crowd.

Chapter Four

The marketplace was bustling and bright. After settling her father into their double rooms at the Shepheard's Hotel, she collected some money (Verity kept all of the household accounts) and asked a shy bellhop in the elevator to be directed to where she could find a few necessities.

Bright scarves fluttered in the stalls, dyed every color imaginable, and embroidered with luminous beads that beckoned to her, winking in the sun. Passing stalls of jewelry, she fingered a pair of brass earrings linked with coral and turquoise stones. The woman behind the counter attempted with all of her well-practiced acumen to press them upon her, but Verity shyly shook her head and stepped back from the stall.

As she did so, one particularly entrancing bracelet caught her eye. Half of her longed to examine it more closely, the other half paralyzed by her fear that the shopkeeper would take offense when she knew full well in her heart that she had no extra funds with which to make such a frivolous purchase.

Moving further on, deeper into the marketplace, she saw fewer tourist-attracting artifacts and more goods that were akin to the necessities she sought. Curving her way throughout the market like an undulating snake, she, at last, made all of her purchases. Tucking her bundles under her arms, she made her way back through the items that had so fascinated her upon her entrance into this strange world.

Once again passing the jewelry stall, she noted that the owner was distracted with a set of American customers who were loudly haggling over the price of some particularly frightful pieces. Taking her chance to examine the coveted bracelet, Verity stole to the edge of the stall and, reaching out, grasped the trinket.

In the center was a single, ornately carved scarab beetle. A common creature from the looks of the surrounding baubles – but the back and wings of it were so dexterously chiseled, the sea-colored stone sparkled in the sunlight. Considering the other, cheaply made artifacts that the woman was also selling in the stall, Verity could not believe the jewel to be precious. However, it was polished so lustrously that a thrill went through her as she turned it to and fro, watching it glint gloriously.

"Oh, daaaaahling. That *is* a treasure!" said a familiarly breathy voice behind her.

Quickly placing the bauble back on the table, she turned to confirm her suspicion. It was, as she suspected, the woman from the train. Verity recognized that several scarves from nearby stalls had been added to the woman's already superfluous collection swathed around her neck. It was almost as if the lady's magnetic presence somehow attracted them to her person as she walked through the marketplace.

As though reading Verity's mind, the woman said, "Oh, yeeeeasss! Do you like them?"

She ran her long-nailed fingers across them satisfactorily. "I absolutely could *not* resist, my dear little dove! The craftsmanship upon these is simply superb! And the feel of the materials – just toooouch that, won't you? It's absolutely luxurious!"

The "little dove's" eyes widened at the stranger's perspicacity as she obliged the request.

"Yes," Verity faltered. "They're very lovely."

"And I'm certain you can't resist *this* trinket, can you?"

The woman gently took the bracelet and admired it much as Verity had herself.

Suddenly, the woman's gaze became a bit unfocused. Pale and wan, she seemed to see something beyond the marvels of the milling people and colorful stalls.

Her eyes, shifting nervously from the bracelet to the woman's face, Verity stood there for several long moments before reaching out and touching her arm gently.

Shaking herself, the woman seemed to come out of her trance and said, in a calm, high voice, "Well, if you're sure..."

Verity looked behind her. She was certain her companion was speaking to someone standing behind her. However, when she turned to see the person, there was nothing but a wall of woven, patterned rugs belonging to the stall next door.

“Sure about what?” Verity inquired uneasily.

Suddenly, she wasn’t entirely satisfied that the lady before her was quite sane.

“Oh, nothing, nothing,” the woman waved a vague hand in the air above her head as though ridding herself of a pesky fly or two.

Then, spinning on her heel, she shouted, “I heard you the *first* time!”

Still puzzled, Verity said gently, “Are you feeling unwell? I’m sure we could find you a glass of water…”

“Water?!” she spun back around and came nose to nose with Verity, scrutinizing her through squinted eyelids.

Verity held her breath in anticipation of…she knew not what…but did her best to hold the woman’s gaze.

Relaxing momentarily, the woman said, “No, no, I always prefer sherry whenever I can.”

The woman began to move away, but Verity called after her, “But the bracelet! You haven’t paid for it!”

Finished with her American customers, and, with a fat wad of cash in her hand, it was the stall owner’s time to peer at the pair of women suspiciously.

“Oh, yes! I nearly forgot,” said the lady casually, stepping back toward Verity. “You simply *must* have this bracelet, my little dove. I just know that you were *meant* to have it.”

She pressed it fervently into Verity’s hand, who thrilled at the cold touch of the metal.

“It *is* rather beautiful,” stammered Verity. “But I’m afraid my father would never approve of me spending money on a treasure such as this without his express permission.”

“Oh, it cannot be *that* much,” returned the woman. “Let’s just you and I see about it. It never hurts to ask, now, does it?”

“I suppose not...” said Verity uncertainly, but before she had finished speaking, the woman had shoved the other customers aside, drawn Verity up to the owner of the stall, and begun haggling for the purchase of the scarab bracelet.

Triumphantly, money changed hands, and the woman pressed the trinket into Verity’s own trembling ones.

“Thank you so very much,” she said, looking up with astonishment into the lady’s eyes, “But I can’t accept this. I don’t have any money to pay you.”

“It’s a gift, my little dove. ‘Twas positively *made* for you.”

The woman gave a knowing nod focused slightly behind Verity’s left ear. With another quick, self-conscious glance behind her, which afforded her no clarity into the woman’s strange salute, Verity felt speechless with gratitude.

“But I don’t even know your name,” she said.

“Vamelda Anstruthers,” returned the woman, smiling

at her widely with gleaming teeth between artificially reddened lips.

"It's extremely kind of you, Ms. Anstruthers."

"Ms. Anstruthers? Nonsense! Call me Vamelda. And *you* are Verity, my little dove, aren't you?"

"Why, yes, how did you…"

"I hope you don't mind me calling you my little dove? You just seem so like one – so innocent."

"My mother, I'm told, used to call me 'sugarplum.'"

"Oh! Sugarplum...I *do* like that. I shall have to use it sometime or other. Well, little dove, I must fly!"

And with that, Verity was left alone in the marketplace, clutching her new treasure tightly in her small, hot palm.

Chapter Five

The riverboat lazily meandered down the Nile – a much slower-moving craft than the swift steamer they had taken between England and France. The winding course of this section of the Nile necessitated a lackadaisical pace that made the journey seem more like a leisure cruise than a trip made often for trade between the two busy ports of Cairo and Aswan.

The professor's disappointment with this lack of momentum was a visible struggle of the soul. His eagerness to begin this life-long dream made him kick against the pricks in Biblical fashion. Verity, on the other hand, enjoyed watching the palm trees, little cities, and lush farms drift by as they floated along the historic river.

Verity found herself inadvertently witnessing everyday, intimate moments of the local inhabitants. Barefooted children chased frogs in the paper reeds along the waterside. A lone farmer's skin sparkled in the sun as he diverted water from the life-giving river to his modest plot of cotton. Once, even, she espied two lovers as they exchanged passionate kisses in the dusky light of the ending day. Verity's cheek flushed rosy as the sunset as she turned her eyes away in embarrassment at having looked on for so long.

At times, the haze of the heated desert would make ripples upon the shoreline – a phenomenon Verity had only read about. This new world both scared and fascinated her. Her imagination ran rampant with all of the novelties that surrounded her. Verity's life had been a very limited one, and all of the new buildings, flowers, faces, clothing, and smells had begun to weave an entrancing ambiance that she found perfectly irresistible.

Even her dreams were woven with strange and exotic places that she felt must be the fruit of her new environs. Just the night before, she had dreamt of the bracelet that the woman, Vamelda Anstruthers, had so kindly purchased for her in the marketplace.

Within her dream, she was older, taller...she even felt stronger. She had placed the scarab-inlaid trinket upon her wrist and, catching her reflection in a mirror, twisted the braids of a Nubian wig around her fingers. As she smoothed a bit of green malachite upon her eyelid, she smiled at her mirrored image. Her duplicate had turned to shimmering, dark water...and the dream was gone.

When Verity awoke, she had felt warm and calm. Many of her dreams of late had been made up of nightmares, so she relished the tranquility that accompanied this one in particular. She felt as though her ancestors were speaking to her, giving her glimpses of the rich and historic past that stemmed from her mother.

The professor did not speak much about his dead wife, but the one thing Verity did know was that she was Egyptian. Sent by her parents to England for her education, she met and married the professor not long after her studies were complete.

Often, Verity wondered if it was merely the fact that her mother was from Egypt that drove the professor to marriage in the first place – he seemed so ill-suited to it now. To commune with a bit of the ancient society that fascinated him – to possess this Egyptian woman as his wife – was something Verity imagined would appeal to him greatly. Collecting artifacts was such a hobby of his that Verity always felt it must have spilled over into his marital vows, however much it pained her to think so ill of her own father.

Despite these disagreeable thoughts, Verity always longed to know more about not only her mother, but her mother's ancestry. This journey held a twofold fascination for her: experiencing new sights and pursuing some semblance of a connection with her deceased mother.

Verity's hand reached out to her beaded handbag. Reaching inside it, she drew out a photograph that was encased in an oval, wooden frame. She gazed upon it half with wonder, half with curiosity.

The woman in the photograph shared her eyes, her mouth, the color of her hair, and the arch of her brow. It puzzled her how such familiar features could feel so foreign to her. She longed to know more about the woman in the photograph, but the professor's tone of voice changed violently whenever her name was even mentioned. Verity knew from experience that the less interest and emphasis she placed upon the subject while in his presence would be the best way forward to learning all she could.

At times, colleagues, passing an eye over Verity, would mention the resemblance, but they were met with rigid rebuttals, the professor claiming that Verity was more like his side of the family. The portrait belied his words, but Verity never refuted his claims.

No journals, no records of her at all, had been kept in the house. Verity wondered very greatly how this token of her mother had been left behind when all else was erased from their home and life. Nonetheless, she guarded and cherished it as a sacred relic.

Hearing the professor's complaining tones in the distance, Verity promptly put away the treasure and resumed reading the history book she had been instructed to consume fully before they landed in Aswan.

"This snail's pace will never get us there in time!" Professor Easton repined.

"But my dear Professor, you cannot expect that the ancient Nile herself would speed up on your account alone?" returned a deep, resonant voice that Verity thought she recognized.

"What's the use of these modern contraptions if they cannot bring us there any faster?" snapped the professor.

As the two men neared Verity, she gave her father a

questioning look that he reluctantly acknowledged.

"I...apologize, Mr. Rashidi," he mitigated. "I'm simply eager to continue my research in person. You can imagine, after all these years, to finally be here is quite a triumph. Quite a triumph indeed, and I long to 'dig' into the work."

The professor made a noise that was meant to be a chuckle at his little joke, but the sound came out so infrequently that it was more akin to the "haw" of a mule.

Verity glanced up shyly at Mr. Rashidi. Rather than returning her look as Captain Bardot had often done, the man seemed lost in his own thoughts. With an unblinking gaze, his eyes were fixed upon the professor – his countenance overcast with a sternness that Verity did not like to intrude upon.

The look passed quickly, and a smile eventually broke out upon Mr. Rashidi's features as he turned his attention to Verity.

"Well, young lady, we meet again."

"Yes," was all she could think to say, but a valiant attempt at a half-smile accompanied the words.

"Your father was just telling me of the purpose of his travels. A very fascinating subject, indeed."

"Yes," Verity could have melted through the decking of the boat for embarrassment at her inability to convey more than monosyllabic responses.

Glancing between the professor and the girl, Mr. Rashidi focused his attention afresh on the father.

"Thank you for your time, Professor. I'm sure we will meet again."

With a slight bow, the sophisticated man removed himself from their company with his usual precipitousness.

"Fascinating man, that," Professor Easton said as he attempted, unsuccessfully, to light his carved ivory pipe. "Not as stimulating as that Captain Bardot for conversation, certainly, but fascinating nonetheless. Has some provocative ideas about Englishmen in Egypt. He all but accused me of robbing his countrymen of their artifacts."

Verity took over the lighting of the pipe, accomplishing the task swiftly and deftly, as she'd done a hundred times before.

Without thanking her, the professor took a long draw upon it and continued, "Seems to think that it's none of our business what his ancestors did in the old days. We had a good, old-fashioned squabble about it, but I don't think either of us was swayed an inch. Why, without outside resources, they'd never have discovered their beloved King Tutankhamun! But he seemed to think that we should have left well enough alone. Harrumph!"

"He does have a point, Professor," returned Verity. "You wouldn't like it if he came and began to claim the works of Shakespeare or the Magna Carta, would you?"

With another "Harrumph!" the professor smoked moodily on his pipe as Verity turned over her father's words in her mind.

Her mother, having been taken from her at such a young age, gave Verity strange insight into Mr. Rashidi's feelings. To have something so precious taken from you, even in the name of science and discovery, must be heart-wrenching indeed.

Verity, troubled too much by these thoughts, returned to her ascribed readings quietly, aside from a little sigh that escaped her lips.

Chapter Six

Upon arrival at Aswan, Verity and the professor settled into their apartments at the Old Cataract Hotel. Verity secretly longed to have rooms that overlooked the Nile and Elephant Island, but sadly, her windows faced the bustling city. As she had been taught ever to smother her feelings and desires in favor of the professor's comfort, such disappointments were soon overcome with a more mature resilience than most girls of her age.

Opening her shutters, she gazed out upon the view. The city was dusty and loud beneath her windows. Children huddled over what looked like an engrossing game of marbles. Their cries of triumph or displeasure carried all the way up to her ears. Fruit piled up in baskets made a colorful landscape directly beneath her. Merchants noisily touted their wares to passersby. One such man she followed with her eye. His brightly dyed blue robes, dusty from walking the streets, were still something to take notice of, especially as he was laden with layers of beaded necklaces around his neck. He called out persuasively as he held up a handful of the trinkets to each lady who came in his path.

One such woman, wrapped in an olive-colored headscarf, paused momentarily to examine the man's merchandise. His charm erupted eagerly as she fingered the quality of the jewelry. However, as she shook her head and attempted to move on, he followed after her until she disappeared inside an alleyway that was swallowed up by the shadow of the hotel. Verity felt for him as he returned to the street dejectedly.

However, an imposing procession at the opposite end of the road sent him running as fast as he could to greet it. Indeed, silk merchants, fruit sellers – almost every purveyor of goods crowded to greet the woman who appeared to be at the center of it all. A splendidly colored, apparently tame parrot adorned her shoulder, and her other accouterments glittered as she moved gracefully down the street.

Brushing aside all the other tradespeople, she pointed at the beadseller, and the woman's servants immediately carved a path for him to be able to draw near. Selecting what must have been six or seven lengths of bead, the man was paid by her attendants. He turned away, delightedly counting the money in his palm over and over again as if in disbelief.

As the woman disappeared toward the entrance of the hotel, the excitement was over, and Verity soon tired of the heat of the sun that was now pouring directly into her window. She closed out the noise and torridity and commenced unpacking her portmanteau.

As she finished, a small envelope slid beneath her door. The white, crisp paper stood out startlingly against the dark flooring. In the center was a red splash of liquid that, at first glance, Verity took to be blood. A gasp escaped her lips, and she stared at the contrasting colors for a moment, held by the gruesome sight in both terror and fascination. Blood had always made her lightheaded and uneasy. As she neared the missive, however, she determined that it was nothing more than a seal of scarlet wax.

The seal had been stamped in Arabic letters, which she could not quite make out – partially because she was still learning them and partly because the seal had been clumsily double-stamped, as though in haste.

Verity picked up the note and took it over to her desk in the corner. Seating herself, she searched the drawers. Notepaper emblazoned with the hotel's crest, she observed, was housed in one drawer, a few fountain pens in another, and...ah! There was a gilded letter opener with an image of King Tutankhamun carved into the handle. It was rather elaborate, but Verity relished the intricacies of Egyptian revival style that was so popular these days.

Feeling along the edge of the blade in admiration, she pricked herself – quite by accident. A drop of her blood splashed upon the snowy parchment – a minuscule reflection of the wax seal. Sucking her finger in aggravation mingled with a hint of nausea, she searched her belongings for a sticking plaster before the blood could pool in earnest.

Once she had attended to her finger, she at last settled

in again to her mysterious epistle. Using the knife and smearing the blood from her prick along the fold (she'd neglected to wipe away the excess blood while applying the bandage), she released the seal to reveal its contents.

It was a stately invitation to dinner for that very evening at the home of Mr. Rashidi. She checked the direction, assuming it to have been meant for her father, but no – he had expressly singled her out as the guest and then, almost as an afterthought, had invited her to bring along her father if she would.

If Verity had any chance of attending, she must conceal this fact, as she knew her father's delicate pride would most definitely be annoyed. Very soon, she made her way along the corridor to the professor's room, thrilled with the thought of her first real dinner party. And to be singled out so definitely was a high honor for a girl only just thirteen.

Knocking on the door to the professor's room, she found it open and in extreme disarray – his portmanteau opened the wrong side up, with clothes spilling out everywhere. Papers and artifacts were mixed haphazardly alongside razors, brushes, and the like. Nimbly, Verity began tidying, gently instructing the professor to sit in an armchair to rest. Heaving a great breath of relief and without thanking his daughter, he did so immediately.

Once his belongings had some semblance of order, Verity ventured to broach the subject of the dinner.

"What? A dinner? *Tonight*?" he responded irritably.

"We do not have to attend, Professor. Although it might be considered a bit rude after your making his acquaintance on the boat and having such a diverting discussion with him."

"Rude? *Rude*?" barked the professor. "It's in quite bad taste to not allow a gentleman to settle in for even *one day* before whisking him off to some unknown..."

"It is only a short boat ride, Professor," Verity said soothingly. "Less than a mile down the river."

"That's even worse!" he further complained, "I've been on boats and trains and more boats for *weeks*! And yet, here he expects me to get on another one!"

"We don't have to go. I'll simply write him a quick note, declining, with our thanks."

In a rare moment of perception, the professor looked down at his daughter's disappointed face. Scanning the room, he seemed for the first time to realize that she must have had something to do with its sudden neatness.

"My child, far be it from me to stand in the way of your having a bit of fun. You'll be alright if you go on your own, won't you?"

"On my own? Oh, yes, Professor! I shall do very well, I'm sure."

"It's settled, then. It's only a short boat ride away from here, you say?"

"Yes, Professor. He writes that a servant will accompany me there and back."

"Please make my excuses, then. He can't expect me to recover from my journey, prepare for my extremely important work, and socialize all in one night, can he? But you...you, my child, with your youth and your innocence from the cares of this world, you can cope extremely well."

Verity had a sneaking suspicion that these were the very reasons most parental figures would not allow their children to go unaccompanied to a veritable stranger's home. However, she was so delighted and intrigued by this new life, and particularly by this invitation, that she was eager to experience everything offered to her.

"He says I shall be returned by eleven. I can ask for him to return me earlier on account of your absence?"

"Yes, yes," the professor merely waved his hand indistinctly in the air toward her.

Already lost in a paper he had selected from the neat pile made on the table near his chair, his momentary interest in her had faded into the realms of the archaic.

Thanking him softly, she shut the door behind her and eagerly ran to her room to reply to Mr. Rashidi's invitation and ready herself for the dinner party.

Chapter Seven

The prospect of a young woman's first dinner party is rife with exquisite anticipation. However, whether or not her expectations are ever entirely met can be quite another matter. Verity's claims to the former were woven with intricate delight, no different than thousands of others before her.

A vividly turquoise gown was laid out upon the bed, glinting with thin strands of golden thread woven throughout the opulent material. Tiny beads gleamed upon the sleeves and hem. They often caught her eye as she busily moved about the room. The dress had been purchased nearly a year previously, but Verity had looked upon it for the last eleven months in despair of ever having an opportunity to wear it before she outgrew it.

Trying it on the morning of the party, she sighed in great relief as it still fit her, if only just. Another growth spurt, and it would have hung, untouched, in her wardrobe...to be gazed upon with acute girlish woe.

With every hair in place and even an old pair of her mother's bronze earrings fastened upon her ears, Verity eagerly slipped into the dress. Halfway over her head, it snagged on one of the earrings.

She tugged at it impatiently. It did not budge. She gave it another tug. No movement on the part of the dress was made. Feverishly, she wriggled and writhed, but to no avail. No amount of struggling could unfasten the material from her earlobe – it simply would not detach!

Resting awkwardly upon her bed, her arms askew in magnificent contortions, poor Verity nearly began to cry in frustration. Forcing back the tears, she resolved to gather her inner strength. She would not allow something as silly as an earring to ruin her much-longed-for evening.

With a low, slow intake of breath, she gritted her teeth and gave the garment a firm yank. A searing pain shot through her ear as she heard the earring clatter to the floor.

At last, she was delivered from the entanglement. Expelling her abated inhalation, she pulled the frock on completely, settling and smoothing it as she did so. Longing to view herself fully in the mirror that rested atop the vanity, she surveyed the room to discover something upon which she could stand. Her eyes alighted upon her dusty portmanteau. Tugging it with nearly all her strength, she steadied herself upon it to admire as much as she could of her reflection.

Looking the dress over with a critical eye, Verity studied her full form appraisingly. She had never shown so much bare arm before, and they looked a bit thin and immature. Her face screwed up in thought, her countenance suddenly cleared as a charming thought popped into her head.

Scrambling off of her luggage, Verity opened it to reveal the scarab bracelet. Clasping it on her wrist, she brushed her hair back from her face. A thrill went through her entire being as she felt the cold metal and stone caress her ear and cheek. Bringing it close to her lamp, she admired how it sparkled, even in the dim light. As she did so, however, she noted that between the front antenna and claws, there was a splash of brilliant crimson that she had not noticed heretofore. Studying it more closely, she realized that it was fresh and wet and, as she touched it, viscous.

Blood. It was blood. But where…?

Lifting her trembling fingertips to her left ear, Verity felt the same sticky fluid. Feeling a little faint with the thought of yet another bloody accident, she scrambled for her purse, where she had previously stowed Mr. Rashidi's handkerchief for the evening's upcoming events. As she held it to her ear, the acute pain that had accompanied her earring's fall returned.

Removing the handkerchief, she saw that it was as red now as it had been snowy a moment before. Searching around her feet, she soon recovered the errant earring. As she examined it, she discovered that a tiny fleck of flesh was attached to the trinket. Verity shuddered as a wave of nausea rushed over her. She had always detested the sight of blood.

Every young boy who had ever tried to tease her with snakes and frogs had never succeeded in rattling her. But one particular boy with golden curls and a freckled nose had once attempted to defend her from a bully. The poor child had received a smack in the nose from the elder boy for his trouble. The rush of blood that had accompanied the blow did not give him the sympathy he thought he deserved from the bright-eyed, young Verity. Instead, she was sick all over him, adding insult quite literally to injury for the young, brave lad.

Even now, although Verity knew it was silly to be so upset by such a wound, she was forced to lie upon her bed for a full ten minutes before she regained her equanimity, wondering if she could gather enough strength to make it to the much-anticipated event.

A knock at the door at last roused her, and Verity tried to compose herself before answering it. The bleeding had stopped, and the subtlest scab was beginning to form on her earlobe – nothing too noticeable, she hoped. Quickly, she removed the other earring and tossed it gently upon the bed as she followed the servant out into the hallway.

Chapter Eight

Following the servant down the stairs and out onto the lower balcony, Verity well-nigh forgot the incident upstairs as she admired the prospect before her. The sable-colored, starry night seemed reflected in the grand Nile as torches lined the banks, lighting the riverway. Beautiful, elongated boats, brilliantly painted in golds and purples, cut through the atramentous waters, escorting fine ladies and gentlemen to and fro between parties, houses, and the famous hotel in which Verity was ensconced.

The chatter and laughter echoed to her against the stark, white walls behind her. She paused for a moment, entranced, and had to be called to attention by a rather gallant serving man, sent by her host to accompany her.

Adroitly maneuvering her through the milling crowd, he then dextrously handed her into Mr. Rashidi's boat. As she sat, trying her best to avoid disturbing the balance of the craft, she noted a few other faces she had seen in the hotel and smiled timidly. Far younger than most of Mr. Rashidi's guests, Verity felt out of place and even, despite her beloved dress, shabby by comparison.

Nervously twisting her handkerchief between her fingers, her eyes were in her lap, hoping to avoid the gaze of those that surrounded her. As she studied her blood-soaked kerchief, she realized that she had neglected to change it for a fresh one. Hastily shoving it into her handbag, Verity glanced up furtively at her refined companions, hoping against everything that they had not noticed the gruesome accessory.

No one seemed any the wiser. They were far too wrapped up – quite literally and figuratively – in their fur stoles, fine jewels, and silken lapels – to notice a moderately dressed, unaccompanied, young child.

These distractions lent Verity some freedom to look about and observe her fascinating companions. Although a few of the ladies did seem a bit chilly in the cooling temperatures of the sunless evening, some newcomers to Egypt had obviously overdressed. Seemingly unwilling to part with their luxurious wraps, they instead attempted to fan themselves. Verity observed one woman who, with brows raised in jealousy, kept an attentive eye upon an exceptionally well-dressed young lady. The young woman was draped in a silky, apricot-colored dress accompanied by a fox fur that was far too large for her slight frame. Her devoted male companion fanned her until beads of perspiration stood out upon his own head from the attempt.

The first woman turned to the indolent-looking man sitting beside her (which Verity assumed to be her husband) and began pleading with him to do the same. After an ill-conceived attempt at feminine coercion, the conversation soon became a quarrel. At last, the man took up the fan and gave it an ineffectual wave or two before allowing it to fall apathetically into his lap. The woman's momentarily triumphant and superior look soon faded into one of disappointment. As she reopened her mouth, perhaps to take up the argument again, she was interrupted as a man stumbled violently into the boat.

The same servant who had so courteously escorted Verity moments before was endeavoring to help steady the man. Cursing him for his trouble, the man shoved the servant aside forcefully, causing the boat to rock until a few ladies cried out in fear. The man was discernably drunk and positively rank with the smell of alcohol. Although he blamed his loss of balance on the servant, it was transparent to all on the boat that he had tripped due to his inebriated state.

Verity locked eyes with the servant in sympathy. His eyes crinkled at the corners in response to Verity's kindly look. It seemed he was used to this kind of crude treatment. Verity was disgusted with the man's conduct, particularly as he sat on her dress, and she spent some time and much difficulty trying to reclaim it.

Almost instantly upon taking his seat, the man began leering at the apricot-clad lady who sat across from them. He studied her body impudently, despite the fact that she was already accompanied by the aforementioned amorously attentive admirer.

As they shoved off, the man's shameful treatment of all

and sundry did not cease. He swore at the boatmen, the captain, and again at the servant. Several times, Verity witnessed him sneak a flask from his inner vest, taking loud gulps of it while he attempted, in vain, to hide his actions with his evening jacket.

This deplorable conduct did not abate as they approached the landing to Mr. Rashidi's establishment. Before they were able to dock, a few guests called out a greeting to their host, who stood on the banks to welcome them. The man began his own greeting by launching a string of profanities at their gracious host as they disembarked from the vessel.

"I'm very sorry you've had such great trouble, Mr. Larcher," said the ever-suave Mr. Rashidi. "Come inside, and we'll see what we can do to make your distressing evening more comfortable."

Verity admired the fortitude of their host. Despite her natural reticence, she had very nearly lost her temper several times with the man as his abominable deportment during the boat ride had grown from bad to worse. Resolving to follow her host's flawless example if she came across him again during the evening, Verity passed, with the rest of her companions, toward the stately entrance of Mr. Rashidi's home.

Fringed palm trees adorned either side of the tiled arches that stretched out across the front of the mansion. A large, square turret on the right-hand side seemed to reach up toward the brilliant crescent moon. Decorative spikes shot up from it to the sky, as though determined to pierce the clouds hovering above them.

Verity paused her movement toward the open doors and was nearly overcome by the surreal atmosphere in which she found herself. Was this...could this...be *her* life? Grand houses, swaying palm trees, punting up and down the historic Nile? Momentarily, she lost her breath in unadulterated awe.

Shocking her out of her reverie came a boisterous, yet not unpleasing, voice: "For shame, my good man! Would you leave this young lady out to shiver in the cold?"

Chapter Nine

The woman's thick British accent trilled behind her as a pleasantly plump arm wrapped itself around her, and the fringe of a silk shawl tickled her arm. The manservant who had been so attentive to Verity earlier in the evening appeared before them both, looking slightly abashed at the woman's reprimand. He bowed to the lady and turned to lead them within.

Verity, quite in shock at this unusual proximity to a stranger, looked up into the face of a grandiose lady. Her eyes nearly stung her as she did so, for the woman seemed to be covered from head to foot in glimmering jewels.

A shadow loomed upon the woman's shoulder, and Verity had to blink her eyelids several times before she made out the form of a parrot whose wings flapped violently for a moment before settling itself into relative calmness with a loud, "In the cold!"

Disturbed by the intelligible words that came from this bizarre creature, Verity's attempt at a polite response came forth as a mangled, "Not a bittold."

By which, of course, she meant to convey that her comfort was unimpaired by the slight chill of the desert air, devoid of sun.

The woman paused for a moment with furrowed brows, but then the meaning of the muddled words must have dawned upon her, for her countenance cleared as she said firmly, "Nonsense! It's utterly frigid out here. You should certainly have brought a shawl along with you. I may just have one in the..."

An obsequious maid handed the lady a spare shawl as though the magnificent woman's mere speaking of the words had magically materialized one from the ether.

"Thank you, Linette. You *are* a saint on this very earth!"

The maid blushed and curtseyed, apparently unused to this fervor of praise.

"She's new. Had her over from France just this very week, but she'll do...she'll do quite nicely, I expect."

The stylish woman nodded enthusiastically as she draped the spare shawl around Verity's arms.

"You're too kind," responded Verity in a bewildered sort of way, although at least able to form something comprehensible.

She was not in the least chilly – indeed, the Egyptian nights were veritably balmy compared to those of London at this time of year.

Looking closely into Verity's face, the woman said, "I see that I've offended you. You're being mighty polite, young lady, but you think me officious. Never mind that. You can't be too careful on these nights. The desert can be positively frigid once those British bones of yours have thawed out a bit in the Egyptian sun."

As she tucked the ends of the shawl closely about Verity's chin, she smiled warmly at the young girl. It was then that Verity recognized her benefactress as the generous woman who had made such a pleasing disturbance in the square earlier that day.

"I suppose I should wait to be introduced – decorum and all that, but we aren't nearly so fussy about these matters in the States. When I see a young one in need, I simply can't restrain myself enough to stand upon ceremony. I'm Elizabeth Elsner...no, no...the last one was Montgomery."

Verity twisted up her mouth in puzzlement. She could not fathom how a person could not recall their own surname.

"You can call me Ms. Bethy. I've been divorced enough times that I do tend to get them mixed up. Ms. Bethy will be your best bet. I'm between husbands at present, so it will be easier for both of us if you stick to that. You never know what gallant man is waiting in the offsides, ready for a whirlwind romance with a wealthy woman like me!"

She chuckled to herself hoarsely, coughing a bit as she did so.

"Linette! My cigarette case!"

The clever serving woman had already materialized the case almost before her mistress had finished the request. She had only to ignite the lighter and place the cigarette holder in Ms. Bethy's hand.

Ms. Bethy drew a long, satisfying drag upon the mouth of the golden cigarette holder, which stood out strikingly against the black cigarette.

Verity had never seen a more glamorous woman, except for the occasional glance she had into those mysterious fashion magazines which she sometimes used her pocket money to procure. She could easily have worshiped this larger-than-life goddess as she stood there, wrapped in the inky night, each bead and gem sparkling with every breath she drew.

"That's better," said Ms. Bethy at last. "My physician prescribed these especially. They *are* rather nice. Would you like a drag?"

Shaking her head, Verity blushed a bit that this dazzling woman assumed that she would know how to smoke or, indeed, that it was appropriate for her to do so at the tender age of thirteen.

Shrugging, Ms. Bethy passed her cigarette holder to the other hand and drew Verity's arm through hers, making a bit of a tangle of their shawls at first. Settling them effortlessly, she took a final pull from the cigarette, shook back the hair from her face, and, with exquisite grace, glided into the house.

The macaw, momentarily disturbed by the bustle of the shawls, had flapped noisily, hovering above Ms. Bethy in the air. Verity expected that he might disappear into the sky above them. However, he merely gave a piercing squawk before gliding silently behind them as they entered the building.

Chapter Ten

All seemed pleased to see Ms. Bethy and, by mere proximity, Verity as well. Quickly learning Verity's name from their first awkward encounter, Ms. Bethy introduced her to all and sundry as though they'd been friends since birth.

Ms. Bethy was praised and admired, flattered and fawned over, and the socialite soaked up every moment of it. By the end of the evening, she had three proposals, a man who casually informed her that he planned to leave his wife very soon indeed, and more invitations to dinner parties and social events than Verity could count.

It could be no secret, then, that Verity also joined the troop of acolytes that worshiped at the feet of this charming and stunning woman. Verity heard whisperings throughout the evening of how abominably rich the woman was, but Ms. Bethy needed no enhancement to her personal charms. She was a performance, a movement, and a religion all in one.

Verity was flattered to be her special confidante of the evening. Great haste and trouble were made to ensure that they sat next to each other at dinner, which embarrassed Verity terribly, but nobody ever seemed to impede Ms. Bethy in any of her wishes.

Nobody, it seemed, but the ever-discourteous Mr. Larcher.

From the moment they entered the dining hall, Mr. Larcher ogled Ms. Bethy. From his few, mumbled words to her new friend, Verity understood that they were already known to one other, although she could hardly fathom how.

Throughout the evening, Ms. Bethy slid in and out of his company, and each interaction with him was more distasteful than the last. He pawed at her gown, breathed heavily upon her neck, and, at one point, even attempted to intertwine his fingers through hers. Nimbly extracting herself from each of these encounters, there was one moment where escape did not seem possible.

After dinner, they had adjourned to another room, where Mr. Rashidi began playing the phonograph while a few couples either gathered up the courage – or were just inebriated enough – to attempt to dance. Ms. Bethy's parrot, who went, quite inexplicably, by the name of Bartholomew, began flapping his wings in a frenzy of distraction at the cacophony. All attempts at appeasing him by his mistress were in vain. He continued to let out a string of colorful language that made Verity blush.

"I do apologize, my dear, but he was given to me by a rather charming admiral. Being used to sailors, he can curse with the best of them," was Ms. Bethy's laughing explanation.

Once the dancing began in earnest, Ms. Bethy was, of course, invited to the floor immediately by a dashing – and considerably younger – man. As she was swept off toward the gallant array of couples, she begged Verity to take charge of Bartholomew and find a secluded place wherein she could quiet him.

After a bit of distracting near-misses from shuffling shoes – and leaving a kaleidoscope of feathers in their wake – Verity and her companion at last concealed themselves behind an enormous velvet curtain.

As soon as the drapery enclosed the odd pair, Bartholomew gave over his profanities and contentedly settled on her arm with a mild, "Which way to the gin mill?"

Within the alcove, she discovered a diminutive bench that seemed just strong enough to support her weight. She drew it out ever so slightly so that she could, by turns, peek out upon the dancing couples or peer into the hallway to ensure their continued isolation. Each time she let in a bit of light, however, Bartholomew would recommence his antics. Waiting until he closed his eyes, she carefully began her observations once more.

Verity observed that Ms. Bethy's popularity did not diminish as the evening continued. Sometimes, she would change partners two – or even three – times per song. Verity found it fascinating and exhausting all at once.

After a particularly energetic Shimmy, Ms. Bethy seemed to grow fatigued. The lady had taken a drink from an adorer, extricated herself from the crowd, and walked into the hall near where Verity was secreted.

About to call out to her friend, Verity was arrested from doing so by the sight of an even more inebriated and malicious-sounding Mr. Larcher. Ms. Bethy's face screwed up in distaste as he came toward her. A few seemingly objectionable words passed between them, and Ms. Bethy moved to join the dancers once again. As she turned away, Mr. Larcher grabbed her wrist and forced her against a wall. He made as though to kiss her, but Ms. Bethy's free hand raised up and struck him fully across the face.

The diamonds that entwined her fingers must have been sharp, for the backhanded blow drew blood from Mr. Larcher's skin. Wiping it from his face, he examined it momentarily as though dazed.

Within seconds, he had placed both of his hands around Ms. Bethy's throat and began to squeeze.

Verity cried out in strangled gibberish, her nonsensical words echoed by Bartholomew's awakening screech.

Footsteps echoed from down the hallway, and Verity was relieved to see Mr. Rashidi running toward the entangled couple. Collaring Mr. Larcher, he dragged him violently away from Ms. Bethy, calling to his friends and servants as he did so.

The group of men, although unapprised of the events, followed the host's suit and escorted the drunken malefactor, without ceremony, from the hallway. Verity knew not to what fate Mr. Larcher would come to – whether the police would be involved or if justice would be delivered from his peers. Her focus was riveted upon her new friend, and as soon as the men were out of sight, she rushed to her aid.

Ms. Bethy was neither trembling nor did she seem particularly upset. Verity held her hand, which was cold as ice, and marveled at her tranquil attitude.

“Shall I fetch you some water? A shawl?” she inquired, eager to be of some assistance.

“No, no. Only...stay with me for a moment, will you, Verity? You’re a comfortable sort of person to have around in times such as these.”

By this time, Bartholomew had settled onto Ms. Bethy’s shoulder, and his mistress began absently stroking his feathers.

As jocular and vivacious as Ms. Bethy had been when entertaining her comrades, Verity expected her reaction to be equally hysterical and upset. Ms. Bethy seemed, in contrast, numb and resolved. And although Verity could still see the red marks of Mr. Larcher’s fingers upon her friend's throat, especially where he had pressed the jeweled necklace into her flesh, Ms. Bethy made no move to detach it from her neck.

Bruises began to form even while Verity looked on.

“Here, let me help you.”

Verity couldn’t bear it a moment longer and began to gently unfasten the necklace but struggled with the clasp.

“Thank you, thank you, dear,” Ms. Bethy patted her absently.

“What *can* have overcome the man?” Verity tried to draw

her friend out of herself in her awkward and gentle way.

This scant attempt at grown-up conversation seemed to snap Ms. Bethy out of her trance.

"Yes," she breathed deeply as the necklace was finally disentangled. "I suppose you do deserve an explanation. You see, Mr. Larcher was husband number three. Very rich, but very possessive. He often treated me...as you have seen...and...and...to be frank, he has never quite overcome the idea that I escaped him."

Giving a flimsy, mirthless laugh, Ms. Bethy gingerly touched her neck with her fingertips, wincing as she did so.

"Unfortunately for me, it is not the first time he has tried to end my life. I would never have come here if I'd known..."

At this moment, Mr. Rashidi returned to the hallway breathlessly.

"Are you in any pain? Shall I send for a physician?"

Ms. Bethy shook her head and returned her host's solicitation with her usual brilliant smile.

"I am quite recovered, Mr. Rashidi. My own private physician will attend me tomorrow."

As he neared them, Ms. Bethy deftly unfastened a few pins of her vibrantly red hair. It had been pinned up to look as though she had a fashionable bob, but it was revealed to be long and lavish. The wavy tendrils draped around her shoulders, and she shook her curls adroitly to hide her neck.

Verity noted this deception and was concerned for her friend but said nothing.

"As you desire."

Mr. Rashidi's tone didn't seem convinced, but he was far too much of a gentleman to contradict her.

"I should like to return to my hotel, I think," said Ms. Bethy, a glimmer of her usual self shining through her eyes. "I believe I've had quite enough adventurous encounters for the evening."

"Certainly. I shall accompany you myself."

"Nonsense, Mr. Rashidi. I'm perfectly capable..."

"Pardon my interruption, but it is for my own vanity's sake that I beg you to allow me to attend you to your doorstep. I could never hold my head high amongst any of my acquaintances if I did not see you safely to your quarters."

Ms. Bethy bowed her acquiescence. As she did so, Verity noted that the roots of Ms. Bethy's hair were as dark as her own, and she wondered how the lady could achieve such colors by artifice. She resolved, upon further acquaintance, to discover how she did so...and why.

Chapter Eleven

The knife drew sharply across the throat. Blood. Blood dripping through her elongated fingers. It was easy – like drawing the bow of a violin across its strings. Nothing could be simpler. The dying light in her victim's eye but a flash of pleading before becoming extinguished. She always liked to watch it flicker and fade into obscurity.

She began to clean her blade upon a piece of stark, white linen nearby before commencing a prayer. Her murmurings became more heated, the echoes of her enchantments ringing back, playing around her ears in the tall, rectangular chamber. She reached a fever of excitement as she watched the last of the blood drain into a pool beneath the altar.

Servants beside her rushed in to clean up the remains, admiring expressions in their eyes as they looked up at her. Scorning their adorations, she would punish them later for withholding even a shred of homage to the god

Aten. If only they knew....if only they could fathom the riches that awaited them in the afterlife if they could but persevere in their purpose.

Aside from the necessary sacrifice, the man had thoroughly deserved his punishment.

Looking down, she admired the polished ivory handle and flint blade as she walked through the halls of the temple. Smiling to herself, she watched the light as it played off of both the knife and the jeweled bracelet she wore upon her arm.

Verity awakened violently, instantly reaching for a nearby bin in which to be sick. The thought of all that blood, and her enjoyment of it draining from the poor victim within her dream, made her physically ill. Trembling, she poured herself a glass of water, spilling a good deal of it upon the floor as she did so. The cool refreshment steadied her a bit, although her heart seemed ready to fly out of her chest, so hastily and hard was it beating.

Slipping on her robe, she alighted nimbly from her bed, avoiding the lubricious water upon the terrazzo flooring. Opening her shutters, she looked at first up at the night sky, replete with stars, then down to the city of Aswan, which seemed merely a reflection of the firmament above, so twinkling were the lights below.

As she filled her lungs with deep, heavy breath, her pulse seemed to slow from the shock of her nightmare. The waxing moon escaped momentarily from behind a cloud and caused a reflection of light to dazzle her eyes. Looking down to its source, she discovered it was emitting from the scarab bracelet that was still clasped upon her arm.

The sounds of the city, distant calls to prayer, drinking houses that stayed open until dawn, drunken Englishmen swearing in the streets...all of that hushed to stillness for a moment as Verity examined her bracelet. It was precisely the same ornament that had adorned the wrist of the vicious priestess of her dream. Momentarily drawn in by the fascination of its inherent beauty, she turned it again to the moonlight, and it shone in her eyes blindingly.

Suddenly, she felt the weight of it oppressively upon her skin, and she tore it from her arm, throwing it across the room with a fractious shriek. It clattered loudly upon the floor with a splash in the water from her earlier clumsiness. Shuddering with detestation, Verity closed her windows and crept back under her rumpled covers.

When the feelings of the dream subsided, she regretted her petulant outcry and hoped that she had not disturbed her neighbors who occupied the rooms surrounding her. Trying to wipe her memory of the horrid dream, she willed herself to fall back into what she hoped would be a more peaceful slumber. Soon, however, she heard unusually loud voices and rushing footsteps outside her door.

"I must have awakened the whole household with my perverse tantrum," she mused internally, keeping perfectly still in the hope that no one would suspect her of being the culprit of the noise.

Lamentably for her nerves and hopes, a great, loud knock came at her door.

"Verity? Verity!"

It was the professor.

As Verity had kept her robe upon her in the chilly night air, she was able to quickly scramble out of bed to unlatch the door. Blinking her eyes in the semi-darkness of the hall, she distinguished her father – his nightdress askew and slippers on the wrong feet – standing before her.

"Oh, thank heavens, child. There's been a most unfortunate accident. I was advised to make certain of your safety."

Patting her shoulder clumsily, he sped off down the corridor toward echoes of shouting with an awkward gait, ostensibly because of his problematic slippers.

Slightly embarrassed by the unusual sign of concern and possible sign of affection, Verity wrapped her robe a bit more tightly about her. Seeking an explanation for his behavior and the voices that were growing ever louder, she ventured behind him a few steps to a turn in the corridor.

Standing there quietly for a moment, she listened intently to the sporadic sounds that reached her. A few shadows that were cast on the wall before here seemed to intimate that their owners were gesticulating feverishly. Verity tried to distinguish the language that was still new to her inexperienced ears. She could make out a few syllables here and there.

Sikiyn...that was knife. *Qumash*...that was cloth. And finally *almawt*...that was...

Death.

Venturing down the hallway in earnest in her bare feet, Verity crept closer to the tumult. A group of men and women were gathered around a door that stood ajar. The professor seemed to be in conference with Mr. Rashidi and one or two other gentlemen Verity recognized from the dinner she had attended earlier that evening.

Verity wondered what Mr. Rashidi could be doing there so late, as she assumed he would be blissfully asleep in his own home at that time of night.

Not a soul seemed to pay her the least bit of attention as she drew closer to them. Her foot pressed against something cold in the dark. Jumping back, she bent down to discover a gilded lighter. Holding it tightly in her hand, she looked up to find that she was being observed by a uniformed policeman in a tall, round tarbush.

He gestured for her to come near him. Obediently, and with bowed head, she moved forward. Gently taking her hand, he removed the object from her possession. She gave it over with no objection.

Now very near the door, she was able to venture a look under the man's shoulder and in at the cause of the commotion.

Just as she did so, Mr. Rashidi called out in much perturbation of spirit, "DON'T!"

But it was too late. Verity had seen it.

The blood.

The gaping wound at the throat.

The man's vacant eyes, that stared straight through her into nothingness – exactly the same as the eyes of the dead man in her dream.

The corpse was none other than the repugnant Mr. Larcher.

Chapter Twelve

A tall woman stood on the precipice of a sand dune, her hands shielding the blazing Egyptian sun from her eyes. A flock of flamingos seemed to have been spooked by some immense creature writhing in the water – more than likely a greedy crocodile. She followed the birds with interest as they circled back around and settled into the river once again, mere yards from what had so disturbed them minutes before.

Verity – for it was indeed she – allowed a little smile to cross her lips, drawing a parallel between the rosy birds and human nature. Much of the time, we ignore the danger of something that so closely touches us...and for what reason? Relief that the peril, though so near, is not entirely focused upon us? Or wilful ignorance as to our real exposure to evil? Only the gods could be privy to such intricate inner workings of the human mind.

Once, she had witnessed a herd of Nubian ibex drinking thirstily from the river. A young kid removed itself from nestling in his mother's life-giving milk and wandered toward the shimmering surface of the water. Looking down curiously, it played fetchingly with its reflection... until that reflection became a mass of sharpened teeth and gaping jaws. The herd ran rampant – kicking and flailing their horned heads about like crazed zealots at some ancient festival.

However, as the water and sand settled, the herd soon calmed and began drinking again in the same watering hole in which the baby ibex was still writhing, calling out to its mother in pain and despair.

Turning back toward the camp while she mused upon such mysteries, Verity began taking long strides in the sand as it spilled in front of her down the dune. On her way up, the sand had been a torrid and strenuous chore to ascend. Despite the arid rays beating down upon her, the view had been well worth it after a long day fastidiously agonizing over the brushwork needed to uncover ancient relics...or what more than often turned out to be not ancient at all. Verity paused to remove her boots and stockings, then continued her nimble trek down the dune, relishing the now shadow-cooled sand as it fell away before her and curled up between her toes.

As she neared the dig's encampment, she noticed that a fuss was being made over a cloud of dust that seemed to be approaching from the distant desert. The noisy bustle of servants and officers was making almost as much of a cloud within their small community as the one that was wending its way toward them. Verity stopped one of the men to inquire about whom or what was expected.

"'Tis *she*! 'Tis *she*!" was all the response she was afforded –

and with little ceremony at that.

Shrugging off this incoherent rejoinder, she moved through the maze of the camp toward her tent. A few archeologists wandered about as if lost in the kerfuffle, confused as to why their directions were not heeded. Amongst them, Verity found the professor. Without a word, she took him by the arm and steered him in the direction of their neighboring quarters.

Once they arrived, she settled him into a comfortable chair, removed his glasses – which were even more askew than usual – dusted them off, and righted them upon his nose.

The Egyptian weather had made the already timeworn wrinkles of the professor's face deeper and more pronounced within the last ten years. His hair and beard had lightened, at first with the rays of the sun and then with the difficulties of his – as yet – unfulfilled goal.

For, despite a decade of continuous searching, studying, arguments, and near bankruptcy, Professor Columbus Easton still had not detected the resting place of his long-sought Queen Nefertiti. Their last sponsor's money had just given out, and Verity speculated that the mysterious dust in the distance could very well be a messenger whose news would ultimately recall them to England.

First, the money from the British Museum had run dry. A strongly-worded letter from that eminent establishment had made its way to them, dismissing the professor in no uncertain terms and blaming him for wasting so much time and money on the fruitless endeavor.

Soon after, however, they had disinterred a modest cache

of jewelry that proved to be dated at approximately the same time that Nefertiti had reigned. This discovery sparked the interest of a South African diamond baron, who made his way to their location and, after studying the beautiful relics, offered to fund the expedition.

The professor naturally sent a vicious letter back to his compatriots at the Museum. He denounced their cynicism and doubt with the most vigorous words (many of which Verity, as his scribe, convinced him to tame into ones that denoted rather less venom than he expressed verbally). Ignoring their dismissal, he violently tendered his resignation from their employment and promptly put his trust into this heretofore unknown man of wealth.

When nothing further was unearthed for several months, the South African gave way to a German archeologist and his wife. Regrettably, the wife and the professor's opinions on Verity's education differed so radically that the money was gone nearly as quickly as it had appeared.

Next, there was a long stream of private donors as the professor sent various letters, and sometimes even assistants, back to England to plead for more time and resources.

The professor very nearly sent Verity once, but the imprudence of dispatching her all alone was pressed upon the professor's mind by Mr. Rashidi, who still visited them from time to time. The professor still did not quite comprehend the difference between his daughter and the other assistants with whom he surrounded himself, but was at last assured that it was the best course of action to keep her by his side.

Verity often wondered if she should be proud that he thought so highly of her ability to work or saddened by the realization that he would have easily parted from her for months, thinking nothing of her safety. But such was the nature of their relationship, and, indeed, it had always been so.

The most recent plea for funding had found its groveling way once again to the British Museum, and the professor, with Verity's usual assistance, had penned a sufficiently humble missive that threw their plight upon the mercy of his fellow academics. Whether or not the professor admitted it aloud, Verity strongly suspected that the rejection of this plea would mean an end to their search for the coveted tomb.

Luckily, the workers had lately unveiled some promising pottery and tools from the purported era. Reluctantly, the professor had sent them along with the letter, convinced by his daughter that such a pledge would do far more than mere words.

When Mr. Rashidi heard of this, he came out to the camp especially to bewail what he considered thievery of his country's artifacts. Verity was inclined to agree with him, but the feelings of duty toward her father that lay upon her heart were far stronger than any amount of argument or persuasion could do to make her act differently. Besides, she had already sent the pieces to England when Mr. Rashidi had accosted them with reprobation for their decision.

When Verity had settled the professor into his chair, she meekly inquired if he knew to what the dust cloud portended.

"Dust cloud? Is there a caravan or just a rider? If there's a dust cloud, they must be on horseback, for we're not expecting anyone of note. It *must* be a telegram from the Museum. I'm sure of it," the professor claimed, setting his glasses askew again in his eagerness. "They *must* have seen from our last discoveries that we are close! So very close!"

Ignoring Verity's remonstrance over having scarcely taken him away from the hullabaloo, he tore out of the tent with childlike avidity. Making his way to the makeshift roadway between their encampment and Aswan, Verity hurried after him with an internal groan of frustration, albeit owning to herself that she was every bit as curious as the professor as to their mysterious visitor.

As the two of them approached the road, a resplendent caravan of camels met them in almost perfect synchrony. Verity drew in her breath at the sight of such splendor.

Each animal was adorned with dangling, dusty tassels fastened with jewels that glimmered in the dusky light. Every saddle was painted in silver and draped in azure fringe. Each man seated within was bedecked in a glorious uniform of coral, while pieces of their ivory turbans draped gracefully across their faces and scimitar swords hung idly by their belts.

This intimidating and appealing site gave way to a dazzlingly decorated howdah, mysteriously veiled with folds of gossamer curtains. As the convoy halted, several of the uniformed men adroitly dismounted and placed together, like a jigsaw puzzle, what appeared to be a set of stairs. One of the men, taller than the others, ascended these stairs and pulled back the drapes.

A much-bejeweled, plump hand reached out and grasped the proffered arm of the uniformed servant, and as the woman emerged, Verity sharply drew in her breath.

Chapter Thirteen

"Verity Easton, as I live and breathe!" said the resonant, familiar voice.

"Live and breathe!" was repeated by a high, nasal tone.

"It can't be!" exclaimed Verity, pleasure exuding from her delighted utterance.

For there before her, blocking the mighty Egyptian sun itself, was Ms. Bethy – the ever-present Bartholomew resting upon her ample shoulder.

Already a middle-aged woman when first they made their acquaintance, Ms. Bethy's amiable face was now creased with a few more wrinkles. They served her well, however, and gave her the look of a woman who had enjoyed laughter and the outdoors.

The two women embraced. Verity was quite as tall as Ms. Bethy, and they made a striking pair as they stood together. Both spoke at once, then paused, laughed, and embraced again. They acted as though they had spent the past ten years side by side rather than continuing a scattered correspondence combined with the occasional chance meeting when the professor's business arrangements demanded a brief trip to Cairo.

"Now," said Ms. Bethy, taking Verity's arm. "Show me your living arrangements. Have you become quite the little adventurer with this rough lifestyle? How have you survived living amongst all these men for so many years? Have you discovered anything thrilling since your last letter? How is your father?"

When Ms. Bethy paused for breath, Verity laughed in response.

"You can't possibly expect me to tell you all of that, can you? I'm hardly used to talking at all, let alone making amusing conversation for a lady such as yourself, Ms. Bethy!"

Pausing, she looked around for the professor, but he was already halfway back to his tent, apparently uninterested in anything that didn't strictly have to do with the dig.

"My apologies, Ms. Bethy. He is so very...busy...and, and..." she paused, searching for the right word, "...preoccupied at the moment."

Verity was stiff in her apology, embarrassed for the professor's lack of civility.

"Well, if you're going to take that formal tone with me, Verity Easton, you might as well address me as *Lady* Elizabeth."

The response was delivered with a playful twinkle of the eye.

"You didn't!"

"I did!"

"The baronet?"

"Indeed!"

With difficulty, the peeress removed her glove to display the most enormous cluster of precious gems – a colossal amethyst framed in the center.

Studying the ring with admiration, Verity congratulated her friend.

"I really didn't think you'd go through with it after your last letter! I thought he'd behaved too abominably with that opera singer."

Lady Bethy waved her glove airily.

"I've always encouraged a modicum of misbehavior in my men. It makes them ever so much more alluring. Besides, how do you think I secured this simply *mammoth* ring?"

She waggled the fourth finger of her left hand at Verity. The young lady, always attracted to jewels, couldn't help but give another trill of approval.

By then, they'd reached Verity's tent. Sweeping aside the covering, she welcomed her guest warmly.

Drawing forth and seating Lady Bethy in the only chair that was housed within her sparse lodgings, Verity bustled about, trying to make both lady and bird comfortable. The bird, she knew, was fond of lupini beans, some of which she happened to have left over from her scanty supper. Bartholomew, delighted, swore heartily in favor of them as he gulped them down his feathered throat.

Verity listened in near silence to Lady Bethy's compelling prattle as the woman detailed every fascinating scene of her nuptials, from the initial buddings of romance to the near division of the lovers to the exquisite reconciliation that was accompanied by the astounding jewel. Verity flitted about her tent, tidying as subtly as she could while giving an occasional nod or murmur of assent or interest.

Verity was not a particularly tidy sort of person. Years of solitude and the sliver of likelihood that anyone would ever see how she kept her lodgings had made her negligent. Hiding an undergarment here, tucking away some dirty stockings there, she did her best to make her apartment a little less disordered for her unexpected visitor.

She had just sat down upon her bed to attempt to ball up a mass of blue material behind her back when Lady Bethy said gently, "Now, what is it you have there, my child? It looks perfectly lovely. Let me have a look at it."

On a recent trip upriver, Verity, unbeknownst to the Professor, had sent away for an evening dress. When a child, Verity was often left to her own devices at the Old Cataract Hotel back in Aswan, where the Professor would meet with colleagues and potential business partners. Bored and neglected, she would enviously observe fine ladies flipping carelessly through fashion magazines as they waited for their friends or husbands. If these illustrious periodicals were ever left unattended, Verity would pilfer them, concealing them in her skirts until she could discover some quiet corner where she could pour over the sensational contents.

Once, the hotel manager caught her doing so. Rather than punish or prevail on the girl's father to reprimand her, he instead had compassion on the wide-eyed child. After that, every time Verity attended the hotel with her father, she would find herself the proud owner of a stack of crumpled but still piquant magazines. Verity would study them as eagerly as a cat licks a bowl of its last dregs of cream.

Although these prizes were often outdated, Verity's most recent trip to Aswan afforded her the triumph of the latest catalog of dresses, straight from Paris. Having little else to spend her pocket money upon, Verity, surprisingly, had enough to procure an evening gown. A simple one, to be sure, but still...from *Paris*!

Unable to have it tailored to her form and lacking any exciting events in her isolated lifestyle, it had never been worn. She had that morning laid it out upon the bed in longing agonies, wishing she would have occasion to wear it someday.

Arranging it carefully in her friend's lap, Verity shyly but triumphantly told her of its origin. Lady Bethy immediately demanded that it be modeled by her young friend.

Verity explained that she had not yet found the means by which to have it tailored. In response, Lady Bethy threw her hands up with a "Pah!" which disturbed Bartholomew so much that he choked upon a lupini bean.

Once the bird had recovered, Lady Bethy stroked her beloved pet as she said, “There is a simple solution. I shall have Linette make a special trip to you. She’ll easily make the necessary adjustments.”

Verity’s eyes glowed with pleasure as the gratitude she felt spilled over in more words than she’d spoken all evening.

“Why, Ms…*Lady* Bethy, I can’t thank you enough! You’re too, too kind to me. You’d really send her all the way out here? Just for me?”

“Why, of course, Verity. There’s simply nothing she can’t do. Her mother was a seamstress, so she knows her way around a waistline and a good hem, although I expect you won’t need yours pinned up – you’ve grown so tall.”

“Oh, Lady Bethy!” Verity clasped her hands and looked upon her benefactress with innocent devotion.

“And then you must wear it to a special dinner I’m giving,” the generous friend elaborated. “You and your father shall come to Aswan tomorrow especially.”

Blushing a bit at the awkwardness of the situation but desiring to disabuse her friend of any unrealistic expectations, Verity returned, “You’re very kind, but the professor will never leave the dig. He only ever goes away on business – never for pleasure.”

“Your ‘Professor’ will for this one – for *me*,” Lady Bethy said assuredly, arching a single brow as she balanced a cigarette at the tip of her holder and lit it deftly.

Unwilling to fall out with her friend, Verity gave a slight shrug and considered that Lady Bethy would soon find out for herself how onerous her task would prove to be.

"And when you come, you must wear all of your finest things, my little dove."

Verity started at the sobriquet. Only that woman – that Vanessa or Vamelda something-or-other – had ever called her that before. The woman who had so kindly purchased that bracelet for her.

"Did I espy a jewelry box somewhere on that mass of clutter you call a vanity? There must be something in there we can liven this frock up with."

Standing and moving over to the aforementioned vanity, cigarette smoke slightly impeded Lady Bethy's search. As she coughed and waved the white wisps of vapor away, she, at last, happened upon the item she sought. Opening the lid, she revealed the very circlet of which Verity had just been thinking.

"Oh, *yes*, my dear – the very thing!" Lady Bethy exclaimed as she pulled out the scarab-inlaid trinket. "This greeny-blue will go beautifully with that netting at the base of your gown."

Holding the shoulders of the garment up for Verity to grasp, she spread the flowing skirt out upon the floor, then moved to place the trinket on Verity's arm, then stood back, admiring the effect of the two together.

As the bracelet's cool metal touched Verity's skin, a shock of delight convulsed through her, giving her a strange sense of elation.

"Oh, Lady Bethy! I am *so* looking forward to it. You're too, *too* good to me!"

"Nonsense, my dear. It's the least I can do for a poor little mite like you, stuck in this lonesome desert wilderness!"

Verity was almost wounded by what sounded like pity from her friend, but the smile twitching at the corners of Lady Bethy's mouth eased her feelings once again into gratitude and tranquility.

"I think it's high time you took me to see your father. I have that invitation to extend."

Lady Bethy stubbed out her cigarette on a nearby tent post and swept aside the tent door flap. This brusque action sent Bartholomew into a paroxysm of profanity as the plate of food he was investigating crashed to the floor. With no time nor inclination to clear the mess, Verity laid aside her dress, took up a lantern, and followed her friend's long strides into the dusty evening.

Chapter Fourteen

Verity still had no idea by what means she'd done it, but Lady Bethy had somehow convinced the professor to dine with her in Aswan. Wondering – yet thrilling – at the tidings, Verity could sleep but scantily as she anticipated what the morrow would bring. It had been many years since she had attended a social event of this caliber. Indeed, the last was that fateful night when Mr. Larcher had met his gruesome demise.

Turning these thoughts over in her mind the next day, Verity styled her hair in preparation, propping a copy of Maclean's magazine in front of her to help her aspire to achieve the desired effect of the curls the ruby-lipped model sported in the center spread. Long ago, Verity had sent by post for a Marcel hot curling iron. Aside from the few times she'd used it in private when it first arrived, it had fallen into neglect, collecting dust and sand, used to prop up a pile of books and magazines.

With one hand, Verity twisted the last unruly hair into

place, while with the other, she set the tool down upon its tiny, gas-powered heater. Searing pain rushed through two of her fingers. Distracted by her hairdressing efforts, she had misjudged the placement and touched the heater by accident. Sucking them like the child that she still was in many ways, she gave a grunt of annoyance.

Turning the pages of her magazine, she recalled a strange article detailing the efforts of a doctor who had shaved, burned, and then tested cures upon rabbits. Feeling sorry for the tiny creatures, she had left the article unfinished in disgust, but her recent pain now left her curious as to the nature of the most successful remedy. Ah – there it was: cloth soaked in tannic acid.

Over the years, Verity had collected quite a cupboardful of handy pharmaceuticals. One-handedly rummaging through her medicines, she ferreted out the little box of powder, along with a short bandage. Awkwardly pouring water from her heavy pitcher into a small glass, she stirred it until the powder dissolved. Verity then dipped the dressing into the solution and gingerly wrapped it around the burn.

A call came from outside her tent. It was nearly time for her to leave for Aswan and the dinner at the Old Cataract Hotel. Linette had indeed made the promised trip that very morning to tailor Verity's dress to the precise specifications of her form.

With no female servant to help dress her, the gown, now in relatively narrower proportions, was quite challenging to place upon her person. Between the hurry of readying herself in time and the predicament her bandaged hand created, she felt a stitch rip under her arm just as she began to settle the netting over her hips. Swearing in frustration with curses that would do Bartholomew justice, she studied the damage critically in the mirror. Lifting her arms, she noted, to her horror, that her undergarments showed through, devastatingly white against the dark garment.

There was nothing for it – she must simply avoid movements that would reveal the deplorable slit.

Attempting to put the laceration of the material out of her mind, she looked herself over and was not displeased at the effect the dress had upon her. Linette had worked wonders with the silken material, and she luxuriated in the way the lamplight glanced off it in starry diagonals. The almost imperceptible bit of white material under her arm was the only damper to her utter enjoyment of the image she made in the mirror.

Shrugging her shoulders as a show of internal capitulation to the fates, she quickly put on her jewels – a pair of malachite earrings (a meager inheritance from her mother) coupled with the scarab bracelet – and rushed out into the night.

Internal trepidation seeped into Verity's veins as she neared the boat. Arriving at this prestigious event with scorched flesh and a torn dress suddenly made her feel highly inelegant.

Although she and her father were the first guests to board the boat sent for them, they were not the only recipients of invitations from their hostess. The boat collected stylish and stately persons as they punted up the river. Each seemed to be more elaborately dressed than the last, and everyone, Verity felt, was markedly judging her. It was remarkable how similar this night felt to that night more than a decade ago, with all of the feelings of her thirteen-year-old self welling up inside her once more.

Verity kept her hands in her lap, hardly moving or speaking to anybody, even the professor. Lost in his own thoughts, he, as usual, took no notice. When they arrived, Verity attempted to disembark, but would not take the proffered hand of the servant on the dock, terrified that such a reach would reveal the wretched rent in her raiment.

Instead, arms clenched stiffly at her sides, she chose to make a sort of awkward leap onto shore as she had seen many a desert rat do. She managed it – only just – and stumbled into the arms of a tall man in a captain's uniform.

Instead of thanking him for his assistance, or even looking up into his face to acknowledge the favor, she turned away and began searching for her hostess. During the debacle, she had felt the seam of her dress rip even more. Attempting to prevent the notice of all and sundry, she tightened the rigidity of her arms even further as she stalked into the hotel, uncharacteristically leaving the professor to find his own way.

The moment she locked eyes with Lady Bethy, however, all soon became calm again. Verity watched her friend's practiced eye rove over her stance and costume, and she felt herself taken by the hand and steered toward the stairs.

Gilded from head to foot, Lady Bethy was an otherworldly

vision, every bit as impressive to Verity as she was during their first meeting. And although Lady Bethy was playing hostess to upwards of forty very important-looking guests, Verity was quickly swept away to Lady Bethy's grand rooms, where she was placed, once again, into the capable hands of Linette.

By great good fortune, the lady's maid had kept the thread with which she had fitted Verity's dress earlier that day. Soon, Linette began to ready her other instruments in anticipation of the mending.

As Verity walked further into the room, Bartholomew greeted her with a surprisingly complimentary, "What a looker!" and gave a low whistle.

"Yes," said Lady Bethy in response to Verity's lifted eyebrows. "I've decided *not* to include him in tonight's festivities. I want my Verity to enjoy herself tonight, rather than peeping from behind a curtain!"

Already feeling discomfited, Verity only allowed a ghost of a smile to cross her features in response to the irrepressible and well-intentioned jesting of her hostess. Verity had no desire to be reminded of her past diffidence.

Lady Bethy traced Verity's cheek with her finger and lifted up her chin.

"There, there, my dear. Linette will have you fixed up in no time. I shall come to fetch you soon."

She swept out of the room, evidently to attend to her other guests.

Verity stepped up onto the velvet dais in the corner of the room and studied her damaged garment in the half circle of mirrors that surrounded it.

“Just here,” she said to Linette, pointing to the rip that seemed to shine out so starkly from under her lifted arm.

As the seamstress began to expertly weave her needle in and out of the fabric, Bartholomew chose that regrettable moment to preen himself. The macaw lost a brilliantly blue feather or two while doing so, and one such plume floated down past Verity’s nose. Her body promptly convulsed with a hearty and unexpected sneeze.

Steel pierced flesh, and the already unnerved Verity let out a shriek of pain and anger that bespoke a flood of emotions disconnected from poor Linette’s unwieldy tool. A string of expletives worse than those she had earlier spoken to her reflection was unleashed upon the lady’s maid, and Verity surprised even herself with the fervor of her wrath.

The door was thrown open, and Lady Bethy appeared and intervened, sending the teary-eyed Linette away with a kindly pat on the shoulder. Soon, she turned her disapproving eyes upon the already repentant Verity.

“I’m terribly sorry, Lady Bethy,” Verity quavered, heartily ashamed of herself and wishing with all her might that the wicked words had gone unspoken.

Verity’s hostess did not have to make a sound for the young woman to come literally to her knees in contrition. “I honestly don’t know what came over me.”

The soft-hearted peeress took a seat near the dais and grasped both the unburnt and bandaged hands in hers, placing them in her golden lap.

"There, there, my dear," Lady Bethy breathed, patting the uninjured hand soothingly, "You've had a most frightful evening. And the fun part hasn't even begun for you as yet! It must be heartily disappointing."

"It is…it's just...*everything*!" Verity wailed. "My hand – my dress – those people. I've no idea what to say to them," tears began to spill onto Lady Bethy's lap. "And seeing me like this...what will they think of me?"

"I quite understand, little dove," Lady Bethy kissed the slender hand that clung so tightly to hers. "But cheer up. You'll absolutely ruin your mascara."

Verity shook her head, "I'm not wearing any."

Delving into her bosom, Lady Bethy retrieved a handkerchief which was, to Verity's discomfort, then used to wipe away her tears.

"We can't have that. A lady of your age, no matter how much of a natural beauty, cannot be caught *dead* at a society dinner without *la mascara*."

Tucking away the handkerchief, she called out over her shoulder, almost deafeningly, "Bartholomew! *La mascara*!"

The intelligent bird obediently retrieved the desired cosmetic and dropped it into the open palm of his mistress.

"Now, little dove," said Lady Bethy, with her ever-affable smile, "We'll have you feeling like a Hollywood movie star in no time!"

Chapter Fifteen

Feeling almost perfectly recovered as she descended down to the first floor in the handsome metal elevator, Verity set her shoulders back in a little, defiant gesture to the world at large – but most particularly to the company that greeted her as the doors separated. Her hostess soon left her side, begging the excuse of past-due attendance to her guests.

Verity had never witnessed such chic people in such refined adornments as those before her. Women were bedecked with fine linens and jewels. In England, men at parties were a sea of dark gray and black, but here, men rivaled women in splendor. Their elongated robes were woven in the most intricate designs and with a myriad of effulgent colors that glistened in the firelight. For, in addition to the gas-lit lamps that lined the halls, Lady Bethy, in celebration of the ancients, had somehow convinced the owners of the hotel to erect great statues of the Egyptian gods, each of them clasping a torch of blazoning fire.

Walking amongst them, Verity contemplated the jutting beak of Horus, the bared fangs of the jackal-headed Anubis, the smooth feline physiognomy of Bastet, and, finally, the jade-shaded features of Osiris. The flames danced upon the countenance of each goddess and god as Verity passed, tricking her eyes into believing that their visages contorted with pleasure or pain as they surveyed the fine assembly.

A chorus of instruments erupted from a balcony above. A man's mellifluous vibrato soon followed, his voice moving up and down over the notes as expertly and expeditiously as smooth water runs over the rocks of a riverbed. Verity stared up at the fine musician, watching intently as both his voice and his expression transformed nigh unto ethereal.

"It is expressly rude to stare," came a voice just behind her ear.

Starting, Verity turned to see the bemused features of Mr. Rashidi.

"Oh! It's you!" she exclaimed, reasoning internally that the man must mightily relish sneaking up on unsuspecting females.

"Yes, it is me, my child," the man returned. "It is a great pleasure to see you again after such a long time."

Verity made a bit of an awkward half-curtsey, unaware of the social custom that would be merited in this situation. She had met him in passing many times during the intervening years, but not for many months and never at a grand gathering such as this.

A low chuckle escaped Mr. Rashidi's lips, and he bowed back with great fervor and gusto. Noting a slight wink of his eye, Verity laughed at herself in turn.

"I apologize, Mr. Rashidi. I'm afraid life at the encampment has left me altogether without knowledge of the correct manners necessary during this occasion."

"But, I see, not without a keen ear for music. *That* is the great Saleh Abdel Hai whom you listen to with such distinct enjoyment."

"Who?"

"I am surprised you have not heard of him, even in your encampment."

"His voice sounds remarkably familiar. I believe some of the workers may have played his music on the phonograph now and again…but I had no knowledge of his name or reputation."

"Ah, yes. I was astonished that Lady Elizabeth found it in her power to pull him away from his engagements in Cairo for such a small thing as a private party. The demand for his talents waxes to excess. In fact, the king himself has had difficulty obtaining his services."

"Lady…who?" Verity said absently as her attention returned to the otherworldly tones of the famous singer.

"I'm beginning to think that you don't know a single soul at this party, young Miss Easton," rejoined Mr. Rashidi.

"I don't! Merely you and the Professor...oh! And Lady Bethy…*that's* who you must mean."

“Yes, Lady ‘Bethy.’” Mr. Rashidi rolled the sobriquet over on his tongue as though savoring it as much as the champagne he brought to his lips a moment later.

A waiter passed, and the gentleman begged a glass for his young companion. As Verity took her first thrilling sip, they both turned their eyes to the very woman to whom their conversation turned.

The silken robe Lady Bethy wore hugged her curves as she twisted herself this way and that, greeting one guest with her lips while simultaneously giving her bejeweled hand to another, while yet another had the pleasure of meeting her welcoming, green-eyed gaze.

In due course, she returned to Verity and her new companion.

As if she possessed the eerie knack of hearing their previous conversation from across the room, she broke in with a, “Divinely gifted, isn’t he? I had to make some awfully scandalous promises in order to convince him to come away from that theater of his.”

Mr. Rashidi bowed over their hostess’s hand, and as he did so, Verity, for the first time, noticed that Mr. Rashidi’s former dusting of gray about the ears had turned to a frosty white. Surprised at the striking change in so short a span of time since he last visited her father, she drew her attention to his features, which also seemed more wan and worn. Wondering a little if Mr. Rashidi had recently suffered from some illness, Verity soon became distracted once again with the singer whose notes drifted mesmerizingly from the upper floor.

"And you, Lady Elizabeth. I hope you left your husband in good health?"

"I always expect my husbands to pine for me dreadfully whenever I'm away, so I must rebuff your kindly wish and comfort myself with visions of him languishing in longing until my triumphant return."

Bemused by the flirtatious repartee, Verity, with some difficulty, drew her attention wholly away from the entrancing virtuoso and placed it upon the handsome couple before her.

They seemed thoroughly absorbed in conversation – as two old friends meeting after a long absence are apt to be. Drawing slightly away from Verity until she could no longer hear their conversation above the din of the music and the crowd, they looked like two conspirators as they moved closer to each other with every exchange.

Smiles and chuckles were traded like currency until Lady Bethy delivered a remark that brought a grim cloud upon Mr. Rashidi's countenance. Placing his hand roughly upon Lady Bethy's arm, Verity's friend winced in pain.

Alarm and a hint of curiosity carried Verity closer to the twosome, and she was shocked to hear Mr. Rashidi's usually placid, comforting tones hardened with acerbity.

"You will consider carefully before you do anything of the kind, Lady Elizabeth," Verity heard him say.

Reaching out, Verity placed her hand upon Mr. Rashidi's and felt that his grasp was indeed as tight as she had expected. At the young woman's gentle touch, the gentleman retracted his grip but with a steely flash in his eye.

"What nonsense you do talk, Mr. Rashidi. I always do exactly as I like. I thought you knew that?" Lady Bethy's tone was light and bordering again on the flirtatious, but the red marks on her arm belied her seemingly cavalier manner.

Without a word, the man turned and stalked away from the ladies.

"Ah, well," sighed the elder of the two. "I suppose I can't win over every man I meet, can I?"

"Are you alright, Lady Bethy? That looks very sore," Verity sympathetically inquired.

"It's nothing!" returned her friend, pulling her gloves a bit higher up on her forearms in order to hide the blemish.

"I recall another time when you brushed off a man's maltreatment of you," Verity said soberly, "Mr. Rashidi was the one who protected and comforted you then. I am shocked and disappointed at his ungentlemanly deportment."

"Yes, it seems evident that the heroic Mr. Rashidi has entirely altered his opinion of me. I confess I cannot think what has made him so impolite and irritable this evening."

Verity looked after the man, but he was soon lost in the sea of glittering guests.

A servant came up to whisper something in Lady Bethy's ear. She nodded in response to his inquiry. He gestured to another attendant, who immediately sounded the dinner gong. The horde of ladies and gentlemen began moving toward the grand dining room.

Verity hesitated for a moment, but Lady Bethy gently took her by the arm and steered her toward the sumptuous smells of food and drink.

Chapter Sixteen

Verity was a tiny bit drunk when she retreated to an upstairs corner near the balcony. Her head was spinning, not only with the champagne, but also with the throng of faces, hypnotic music, and fascinating conversation she'd encountered throughout the sapid repast.

Earlier in the evening, Lady Bethy had seated her between two rather dapper young men who made shameless advances at her until they learned that she was but the humble daughter of a little-known archeologist. The attention of one was promptly turned to the overeager flirtations of a married woman, and the other continued to make only desultory overtures to Verity whenever he caught Lady Bethy's stern eye.

Lady Bethy and the professor were seated several chairs down the table, their hostess, of course, enthroned at the head. Verity was surprised when she witnessed the professor seat himself to the left of Lady Bethy. After a few whispered words from her accompanied by a touch to his arm, Verity watched the professor's countenance transform from vague boredom to supreme interest in a matter of moments.

A few more whispered words, and she observed Lady Bethy produce a small box from within her ample bosom. Setting it down carefully on the table between them, she used one perfectly manicured finger to dramatically nudge it toward the professor with one swift motion, stopping unexpectedly at his right elbow.

Hesitatingly, he took it up, opened it, and blinked rapidly in what Verity read to be disbelief. Removing his spectacles, he wiped his eyes with his shirtsleeves, then, replacing the glasses, peered into the box for a closer look.

A veritable smile broke out upon his weathered countenance, and Verity, curiosity overtaking her mind, made a mental note to ask her friend or the professor about the odd exchange at the earliest opportunity. Gulping down the remains of his soup, that venerable man excused himself from the table and hurried off to regions unknown.

Verity, longing to follow after the professor but fearing it would be impolite of her to make Lady Bethy lose two guests in quick succession, chose instead to stay seated. No doubt he would return for her later or, perhaps, in his usual absentmindedness, had forgotten about her existence altogether.

Resigning herself to her fate, she noted that across the table, a gentleman and lady were exchanging heated words pertaining to the current politics of the country. Often wandering amongst the workers at the archeological campsite, Verity had heard whispers of discontent about the hold England still maintained over the country. These susurrations would often cease whenever Verity drew near, so her curiosity was again piqued when she listened to the two intelligent individuals.

Catching bits and pieces of their conversation as though collecting flowers for some strange governmental bouquet, some of her suspicions were confirmed, and her heart was torn in two. She loathed hearing the England of her youth disparaged, yet she sympathized with her mother's people and their desire for full independence. For, although the British protectorate had ended decades before, their occupation and presence were still keenly felt.

The lady, noticing Verity's interest, attempted to draw her into the conversation. However, Verity found it a complex subject to navigate in her own mind, let alone in the company of people far more well-versed than she. Shaking her head in declination, she retreated into herself and soon had to fend off the watery eyes of a young man sitting across and a few seats down from her. Oblivious to the nature of her humble origins, he waggled his eyebrows at her in a most incommodious fashion.

When dinner was done, Verity made her way with the rest of the crowd to the ballroom, where the watery-eyed lad swept her up in a dance before she had a chance to politely decline. Between stepping on her toes and bumping into other couples, he plied her with endless flutes of champagne – many of which found their way into the soils of sizeable potted plants conveniently placed nearby.

At last extricating herself from the young man, Verity stumbled her way up the stairs and into the aforementioned secluded corner away from the crowds. After resting against a steadying column, she closed her eyes for a moment and slid to the ground, turning her head ever so slightly, so the cool marble could just touch the back of her neck.

Unexpectedly, she fell almost immediately into her dream. This time, however, the romance and fascination of her current surroundings shadowed her as she walked amongst the paradise of this familiar realm. It was as though the two worlds had merged, and she could hardly tell the difference between them.

In the dream, however, she was alone. Gliding silently amongst the tall statues of the gods and goddesses she had in reality seen in the hall, a simmering rage began to effervesce inside of her. From whence that spasm of fury stemmed, she could not tell – she only knew that she must express it – set it free!

She began running – faster and faster – until she leaped upon the table where the feast had been laid. Taking up a tureen, she smashed it on the ground. Kicking the fine china onto the floor, she felt a delicious sense of satisfaction as she watched it crack into a million pointed shards.

Next, she rushed over to a statue of Thoth, pressing her body against it until it toppled over with a great crash. The elongated beak of the ibis-headed god broke with the weight of its fall, while the flame of the torch flew out of his hand and landed upon a curtain.

Blazoning fire reflected in the eyes of the perpetrator, and she laughed with maniacal glee. Gathering up several bottles of champagne, she hurled them with full force at the face of Osiris. The countenance of the great god of the underworld became distorted with burgeoning cracks until...

Something disturbed Verity from her nightmarish slumber. Was that the sound of retreating footsteps echoing down the hallway? Pulling herself from the floor with difficulty, Verity shook her head with the intoxication of both drink and dream.

Wandering toward the balcony, she noted that the band had abandoned their instruments and chairs, evidently for a brief respite. She became momentarily fascinated by the instruments, having never had the opportunity to view anything of the kind in such close proximity before. Tenderly caressing the cymbals of a tambourine, the soft leather stretched tightly over the drums, and finally, the slender neck of a lute, she was fascinated. Sliding her fingers lightly along the strings, she noted that one had been broken off. Verity smiled to herself at what she supposed was the musician's fervor at the performance of his art.

Verity had seen photos of her mother playing a lute akin to the one before her. Sighing, she imagined the life that could have been had her mother lived. She pondered whether her mother would have passed the gift of music on to her daughter.

Feeling sorely neglected, Verity wished more than ever

in that moment that her mother had been by her side to teach her many things besides the music she was daydreaming of now. She often felt naive and inadequate – the awkward dancing and horrendous embarrassment over a simple conversation with young men of an eligible age were but two examples of her keenly felt shortcomings.

At least she had, for however short a span of time, the guiding company and friendship of dear Lady Bethy. Kind, generous, full of life...Verity determined that she would try her best to emulate her friend, especially now that fate had brought them into close proximity once again.

Thinking back on her previous incivility to that very woman's lady's maid, Verity's cheeks suddenly splashed with flame at the remembrance.

Determined, even in her slightly inebriated state, to make a full and profound apology to Linette, Verity made her way, by help of the steadying walls and columns, down the hall to Lady Bethy's apartments.

Quite dizzy and breathless when she arrived, Verity waited just a moment outside of the doors, gathering her thoughts. Realizing that Linette could very well be in her own chambers instead of in her mistress's, Verity nevertheless knocked firmly on the doors on the off-chance that the lady's maid happened to be there, preparing for Lady Bethy's return.

As she knocked, the door swung open, revealing a flickering lantern in the corner. As Verity's eyes focused sufficiently, she noted that the lantern was lying on its side, spilling out oil from the dresser onto the carpet. A small flame began to lick just outside the glass and began to follow the beckoning trail of oil.

Expeditiously crossing the room to set the lamp upright, Verity seized a nearby shawl, covered the burgeoning blaze, removed one shoe, and used it to stamp out the fire. As she gingerly peeked beneath the blackened cloth, she let out a grunt of gratification. The fire was out, and all was well.

No sound came from Bartholomew, over whose cage a coverlet had been laid, evidently to quiet him for the night. Verity was surprised that he had not stirred, as the fall of the lantern must have made some amount of noise. She moved to lift the material to ensure his safety, but as she did so, she glimpsed a reflection in the wide mirrors.

Linette was curled up, catlike, on Lady Bethy's bed. Verity chuckled under her breath. She thought of the poor woman, more than likely overworked in the preparations for the party with the added strain of mending Verity's dress at the last minute. She must have prostrated herself to steal a moment's ease but then fallen into a well-deserved sleep.

Verity hoped to make up for her previous ill-usage and resolved to awaken the slumbering maid before her mistress detected her presumptuousness. Turning and moving over to the bed, Verity gently shook Linette's shoulder.

The woman did not move.

She shook it again and softly called out, "Linette."

Still no answer.

Verity shook still more firmly, and Linette's form flailed limply at the more potent touch, rolling from her side to her back, her eyes wide and staring.

Jumping back, Verity exclaimed, "Oh! Linette. You frightened me. Get up! Lady Bethy may be back at any moment."

But before the sentence finished traversing her lips, Verity saw it.

The thin string of a lute was wrapped tightly around Linette's neck, cutting into her raw flesh, painting a delicate crimson line across her throat.

Chapter Seventeen

In a quiet apartment, far from Lady Bethy's recently vacated chambers, Verity sat with red eyes and a swollen nose. As the police and the hotel manager questioned her hostess, the lady in question held her head high while her face remained virtually devoid of emotion. She answered them logically and effortlessly as if one of her maids was murdered every day of the week.

Verity was quite another story. She sobbed and sulked and surrendered every internal thought (many of them thoroughly irrelevant to the circumstances) to the police until they were unavoidably satisfied that she was utterly innocent of the crime.

Envying Lady Bethy's sense of decorum and self-control, Verity felt each ounce of her naivete to her core. After Verity's most recent flood of tears that rendered her unable to release a single intelligible syllable from her lips, Major Nabil turned in exasperation to Lady Bethy.

The tall, commanding major had been called in especially,

evidently due to the illustriousness of Lady Bethy's position.

"Someone is most assuredly out to get me. I have dealt with jealousies and threats my entire life, but this simply takes the cake!" said she, her voice trembling for the first time since the news had been delivered to her.

"I assure you, Lady Elizabeth, that we shall make all inquiries necessary until we find the heart of the matter," bowed the major.

Verity, despite her distress, observed that he looked like a very shrewd sort of man, and she hoped with all her heart that there would be clues enough to aid him in his endeavor.

Major Nabil continued, "Can you think of anyone who would desire to incur such violence upon this Linette..." he consulted a small, worn leather notebook in his hand, "Linette D'aurevelle?"

He pronounced the French name fluidly and with a perfect accent, which made Verity suspect that he could speak the language very well if pressed.

"Linette knew not a soul here as far as I'm aware," answered Lady Bethy.

"And the opium pipe we found next to her? You had no knowledge of her...habits?"

"It was a complete surprise. She's never mentioned it to *me*," returned Lady Bethy, noticeably affronted but soon recovering herself. "But, of course, she *wouldn't*. That is why I'm convinced that it was intended as a threat to *me*."

"And these jealous individuals...can you name them?"

Verity's friend brushed off the question with a wave of her bejeweled fingers.

"I'm telling you! They are all around me! I do not know which are my friends and which are my enemies. These are the people who would tell me perfectly lovely things to my face yet behind my back – oh! The horrors they speak! I have been threatened..."

Verity's mind wandered back to Mr. Rashidi and the interaction she had witnessed earlier in the evening.

"If you could but tell me the name of those..." continued the persistent major.

"I am quite fatigued. Could we not continue the rest of this distressing conversation in the morning?"

Major Nabil bowed in assent and withdrew – an entourage of officers and hotel staff at his heels.

Once the door closed upon them all, the unseen dam that had apparently kept Lady Bethy's emotions at bay let loose in full flood. Shocked, Verity was soon comforting her friend with a squeeze of the hand and an offer to stay the night with her.

Feeling a little bold at the proposal, she withdrew her hand and instead used it, along with the other, to bury her face. It was Lady Bethy's turn to play the angel of comfort, and she let out an exclamation of delight through her tears and immediately drew her young friend into a warm embrace.

"Of course, you must stay the night, my dear. After all, it

saves me the trouble of pushing these two dreadful beds together! I can make do with a smaller one for the night. I'll send word to your father that you are to stay with me, for I believe he's already headed back to the camp."

Standing up, she called, "Linette! Linette, I need you…"

Lady Bethy abruptly sat down again as she seemed to realize that her calls to the maid fell on ears that could no longer heed them.

Tears recommenced in rivulets down her face, and she looked imploringly at Verity.

"*I* shall send word," Verity interpreted her silent plea as she resolved to take control of herself. "Please take your rest, Lady Bethy."

Verity made her way to the door, then, turning back, queried, "Shall I send for a nightdress as well?"

"Make it two, for you cannot sleep in that thing," the peeress returned, unable to help, despite her distress, looking over the young girl's frock appraisingly with a practiced eye. "Tell them to send for my summer nightdress for you. It's considerably shorter and sleeveless, so it won't drown you quite so much as one of my usual negligees."

Obediently, Verity darted out into the corridor and was in great luck to discover one of Lady Bethy's servants hurrying down the hallway. The instructions were given, despite Verity's blush at the mention of something so scandalous as a negligee, and the serving maid tripped silently away. Not long after, there was a knock at the door, and a neat bundle was delivered into Verity's hands.

She changed rather abashedly behind a dressing screen, yet in full view of Bartholomew's beady pale yellow eyes, which followed her every movement. Verity nearly toppled over when he released one of his signature low whistles as she removed her chemise.

Once the two ladies were settled into their beds, Lady Bethy was just turning down the last lamp and covering the macaw's cage when Verity recollected her intention of inquiring about her friend's conversation with the professor.

"Lady Bethy, forgive me, but what was in that box that you showed the professor during supper? Could it have any relevance for what has transpired tonight? Was it something precious that a thief could have..."

"In the morning, dear. In the morning," Lady Bethy interrupted with a theatrical stretch and yawn. "I'm very tired and distressed now, as I'm sure you must be, too."

The light went out, and Verity hoped that she could find sleep amongst the terrifying circumstances that seemed to surround her in wild restlessness.

Chapter Eighteen

Never before in her life had Verity experienced the sumptuousness of the morning meal before her. Nor had she ever been given the opulent opportunity of breakfasting in bed. She was used to consuming her morning meal alone with only meager portions of tasteless fuul, a gruel made of fava beans. The cook at the camp took no special pains over her food, so she was overwhelmed by this generous supply of tempting victuals. Looking over at Lady Bethy, Verity could see as her friend uncovered her own steaming copper cloche, that no lesser portion had been served to her.

Hot, billowing Baladi bread, smooth, creamy cheese of a pure witness that she had never before set eyes on, a colorful array of fruits that were difficult to procure at this time of year, clotted cream that she did not quite know what to pair with, and, yes, the ubiquitous fuul (with which she was all too familiar, yet this tasted delectably of garlic, coriander, and – was that mint?)

made up her terra cotta tray that simultaneously warmed her lap.

Their attendees treated Verity with the same measure of respect and decorum as her eminent friend. It seemed as though a guest of Lady Bethy's was an honor that drew her far above her usual humble status.

After the servants had brought in the breakfast, they spent the morning filling the wardrobe in the corner with Lady Bethy's expensive-looking clothes. Verity watched them as hungrily as she ate her repast, with just a hint of jealousy glinting in her admiring eyes.

Gorging herself until she felt the stitches of her roomy nightdress tighten a bit around the middle, Verity at last set down her fork and knife. A servant rushed in and removed the tray, giving her a warmed, wet cloth with which to wipe her sticky fingers.

Seeing that Lady Bethy was similarly occupied, Verity was once again eager to bring up the subject of the unusual conversation she had witnessed the night before between her friend and the professor.

Just when Verity was about to speak, Lady Bethy broke in with, "Now, my dear. You have been incredibly patient with me whilst I indulged my appetite for this heavenly food. I know you want to know all about my conversation with your father. Thank you, Kafele. Just place my fawn-colored robe here and open Bartholomew's cage, then you may go."

This last was to a hotel attendant who obeyed Lady Bethy's instructions before shutting the door.

“What a nice young woman. We should speak to her about her education. She’s far too intelligent to be a servant all her life."

Lady Bethy stood and slipped the robe around her voluptuous body. Verity admired the way its ruffles cascaded down to the floor. She longed to feel the silky material enfold her own skin.

Once the robe had been settled to Lady Bethy's satisfaction, Bartholomew fluttered over to her shoulder.

"Yes, my pet," she continued in a cooing voice as she stroked his feathers affectionately. "We'll just have to see what we can do about that."

“Lady Bethy…” interrupted Verity, a tiny bit frustrated that Lady Bethy’s attention had been drawn away from the subject that had been giving her anxiety.

“Oh, yes! As I was saying, you’ve been remarkably tolerant with all of this suspense, and I meant to tell you last night, but I…oh dear.” Lady Bethy sat down upon the bed again, as though overwhelmed with emotion, “I had quite forgotten about last night.”

A stiffened silence cut between them, as though the remembrance was a freshly reopened wound that rendered them speechless as they watched the blood dry upon the knife.

“Poor Linette. Poor, poor Linette,” Verity said, fighting against the tears that welled up in her eyes until her irises turned from deep brown to a luminescent russet.

“There, there, my dear. Let us not dwell on it. We *must* not dwell on it...for now."

Lady Bethy stood again and began rearranging her sleeves, which swept down in widening folds of ruffles. For a moment, Verity looked upon her in awe at her regality. The peerage into which she had married may have been fairly recent, but Lady Bethy had, even before then, always seemed to exude an almost palpable sense of majesty.

"Let us get dressed, and I'll tell you all about it when we go downstairs."

Verity whipped off the covers in eager anticipation of the conversation.

Hurriedly catching up her bloodied dress and crossing over to the dressing screen to change back into it, she was impeded by her friend, "No, no, my dear! You simply *cannot* wear that disgusting thing."

Pain lined Verity's youthful features as she looked upon the ruined frock.

"Here," Lady Bethy said firmly, taking Verity by the wrist and leading her to the broad and impressive wardrobe.

"We shall certainly find you something suitable. Luckily for you, the rage from Paris seems to be a bit of a loose-fitting thingy. Let's just see if we can make something look like that on your figure..."

She pulled out two, then three, mid-length dresses and held them up to Verity's chin.

"With a bit of a tie cinching at the waist, here."

Using a belt, she cinched all three dresses to Verity's

midsection as one. Tugging one after the other out, Lady Bethy eyed the effect of each.

"Yes, I do believe that maroonish one with the pleats will do perfectly. It will bring out that wild reddishness of your eyes that I like to see."

Visibly and emotionally uncomfortable, Verity unfastened the belt and made her way, with the chosen dress, behind the screen to change. Once she had done so, she emerged to witness Lady Bethy stuffing Verity's old dress into the bin.

Horror mixed with immense sadness overtook Verity.

"I know, I know, my darling little dove. It is your only truly chic item, and I know you've absolutely ached for it for ages and all that, and Linette did a stunning job of suiting it to you perfectly, but it can't be helped. Allow me to replace it for you with something better."

Sadness overtook Verity's countenance, predominantly for the memory of the lost Linette, but a tiny sliver, if she was truly frank with herself, over the delicious delicacy of her first and only fashionable frock.

"In the meantime," continued Lady Bethy, "Let us find some little bauble to cheer you up."

Whisking her own lavish nightclothes in a wake of rippling folds behind her, she strode toward her vanity, where she unlocked an elaborately carved, ebony jewelry box with a minuscule key that hung from a lavaliere at her bosom.

With reverence, she removed a few opulent pendants from the rich, inky-colored velvet upon which they lay.

Turning the box halfway around, she lightly pressed the petal of one of the engraved flowers, and a hidden drawer sprang into existence. At the center of it, settled imposingly upon jade-tinted threads of silk, lie an exquisite brooch. It was made in the image of a gilded lioness, teeth bared, as she held a great ruby in her hungry mouth.

Turning to her friend, Lady Bethy pinned it, not to Verity's shoulder as she had anticipated, but in the center of her braided leather belt that held her gown so tightly against her waist.

"There," the generous lady said, stepping back and admiring the effect of her work, "Let that serve as an anathema to all that would oppose you, my dear girl."

Verity traced the cold metal with her fingertips, knowing she should protest at so generous a gift. But the desire – the burning craving – she felt to possess such a treasure was too much for her to overcome the niceties of social convention. That, combined with her upbringing so apart from the society that would surely have trained her for more conventional protestations, gave Verity the liberty to simply take her friend's hand and kiss it with innocent and effusive gratitude.

If Lady Bethy was shocked at this lack of decorum, not one feature of her face displayed it. She merely returned the caress with an equally innocent one of her own as she touched Verity's cheek with a maternal gesture.

"Now, my little dove – although you seem somehow less like a dove with that brazen animal staring out at me – let us speak about your father."

Chapter Nineteen

As the two friends strode through the patterned arches toward the balconies at the front of the hotel, they conversed in low tones and looked like two thieves plotting their next larceny.

In truth, they were speaking about the professor and Lady Bethy's conversation from the night before.

"As you know, my dear little dove," said Lady Bethy as their skirts swished in syncopation while they walked across the cool floors. "Your time in Egypt will soon come to an end. Your father has confessed to me that he has spent every cent of your meager inheritance to fund this dig. I heard whispers that he was not only losing his money but also the respect of his colleagues. Much is rumored about the solidity of his very sanity for spending a decade in what seems to be a hopeless pursuit."

Verity nodded slowly as her friend continued.

"'Bethy,' I said to myself, 'You simply *cannot* let these

rumors adversely affect your little friend. You must exert yourself!' So, I tore myself away from my handsome young husband and came to the rescue."

"I do not understand," Verity said quizzically. "How can you 'rescue me,' as you put it? I don't mind returning to England. There is much I love about my mother's homeland, but I am ready for whatever Life has in store for me."

A little half-smile accompanied by a determinedly thrust-out chin made Verity look the picture of youthful moxie. Lady Bethy smiled at the unconscious performance.

"But you see, Verity," she said, taking a step in front of the younger woman to face her.

The couple had nearly reached the end of the balcony, and as she spoke her next words, she was outlined by the blazing morning sun in utter splendor.

"*I* am going to fund the dig!"

"What?!" exclaimed Verity, astounded by Lady Bethy's continuous magnanimity. "But why would you...?"

"Something of this nature has been on my mind for quite some time. And although I am a very wealthy woman, that alone is not sufficient to make my mark upon the world. I've always had a fascination with the ancient queens of Egypt, and when I heard of your father's plight, I determined that this was the perfect opportunity."

"And what you showed to my father last night...that was something that can help?"

Surprised, Lady Bethy withdrew a step to keenly

scrutinize Verity's face.

"Interesting…yes, I see that you are a sharp observer, Miss Verity Easton. I shall have to keep an eye out for that."

Casting her tongue over her dry lips and smiling, Lady Bethy turned to gaze out upon the gray-green glassiness of the Nile.

"It's time for a drink, I think," she said, a bit of harshness in her voice. "Call for a waiter, will you? I'll find us a cozy corner where nobody will dare to eavesdrop on us."

Verity did as she was bid, and as she seated herself across from her friend, she noted the same little box she had observed the night before. Although where Lady Bethy had pulled it from, she could not fathom.

As her eye was distracted by the box, Verity very nearly missed her chair, so surfeited was she with curiosity. After the jewels and gems she had so recently witnessed as part of Lady Bethy's accoutrement, she was expecting more gleaming baubles and glistening precious metals. As her friend opened the box, Verity let out a harrumph of disappointment. It contained nothing but a dusty shard of red ochre – surprisingly similar to the one that had changed Verity's fate so radically ten years previously.

"What is it?" asked Verity with the disdainful apathy that only youth can conjure in such theatrical tones.

"Oh, how can you be such a bore? One minute, your eyes are shining with curiosity, and the next, you make me feel as though I'm a hundred and twenty! Come now, this must spark some interest in that intelligent brain of yours!"

"I'm sorry, Lady Bethy. I did not mean to be rude, but I've seen simply hundreds of red ochre tablets...*and* dusty old pots *and* broken canopic jars *and* wooden ankhs. I'm just sick and tired of the lot of them! They never prove anything, and then when they're not connected to Nefertiti, the Professor is unbearable for at least a week until one of the men finds something else, then it starts all over again!"

She threw her hands up to the sky in frustration, then, embarrassed at her outburst, slumped back in her chair sulkily.

Lady Bethy laughed, her teeth gleaming as they crunched the rosewater-and-saffron-flavored ice the waiter had brought to their table.

"Well, go on, my little dove. Take a look, even though all of your youthful soul rebels against it."

Verity sighed as she drew the box toward her, making a little scraping sound across the table as she did so. If Lady Bethy was annoyed at this petulant performance, she did not let it show upon her countenance. Instead, she continued masticating the ice loudly, transferring it from one cheek to the other as she studied her friend with narrowed eyes.

Tracing the indentations of the tablet with her finger, Verity gingerly brushed away a bit of the sand as she did so. The symbols were familiar, and the message was straightforward. Verity's eyes flashed up to her friend's with interest when she was nearly to the end.

Lady Bethy merely continued to smile at her, covering

another heaping spoonful of flavored ice with her lips that were becoming reddened with gelidity. Bartholomew gave a fractious squawk, and she paused for a moment, opening her mouth to allow the bird to nibble little bits of crushed ice from her tongue.

He tilted his head back, letting out a pleasurable, "A hearty swig!" as the ice slid down his throat.

Verity didn't even notice this strange interaction, so engrossed was she in the new information the tablet presented to her. When she had finished perusing it fully, she sat back in her chair with a thump. Crumbling a bit of ice between her long fingertips, Verity savored the information as much as the macaw seemed to revel in the frozen delicacy.

"So this means that…" Verity began.

"Yes."

"We've been digging?"

"Yes."

"Then that would mean…"

"Indeed."

"Then you?"

"Naturally."

"It's not far from where we have been looking."

Lady Bethy waved her spangled wrist as they finished their little habit of thought transference.

"A mere fluttering of an expense if what it says on the

tablet is accurate. The treasures her tomb will hold are said to be vast in comparison to that of Tutankhamun. Although her son did not approve of her religious endeavors, her loyal followers are rumored to have filled her final resting place with untold treasures."

Raising an eyebrow, Verity accused jestingly, "Then your motives aren't completely unmercenary, Lady Bethy."

The woman tossed her head as a bit of melted ice dribbled out of the corner of her mouth.

"I think we both know that I'm too far gone down the path of immorality to ever be accused of being *absolutely* pure of heart, but I do have my moments."

Looking down at the lioness at her waist, Verity caressed its head as though it was a live feline and felt a rush of excitement flow through her veins as she did so.

"You certainly do. You're far too generous, Lady Bethy," Verity returned.

The parrot interrupted their conversation with a nibble at Lady Bethy's mouth, hungry for more of the refreshing delicacy.

"Ouch!" said Lady Bethy, shrugging off the parrot and shooing him away from her toward the edge of the balcony. "Blasted bird!"

A bit of blood replaced the stream of melted ice that was dripping down her chin. Verity watched it intently, fascinated by the way the two viscous fluids comingled. A flash of white disturbed her unusual thoughts as Lady Bethy dabbed at the wound with a napkin.

"So what do you think of it all, little dove?" she said expressively, "We're moving to Philae!"

Chapter Twenty

Verity stared at her hands. They were covered in blood – absolutely saturated with it, but she did not mind in the least. In fact, she reveled in it as though it was a luxuriant bath foaming with pungent peregrine perfumes. As she felt the red liquid slip through her fingers, Verity watched herself continue her grisly task.

She was carefully and meticulously flaying a snake.

Completely limp in her hands, she could feel the smooth scales of the reptile peel away from the muscular shape as she forced it into rebirth. Just as she decorticated the last bit of skin from the tail, the creature suddenly grew tense with life and darted its hooded, fanged visage toward her face, teeth bared wide to strike.

Awakening in a sweat of anticipation and terror, Verity sat up in bed with a scream upon her lips. Lamps were lit; footsteps beat a rhythm toward her tent. It was one of the workmen who called to her in Arabic, asking if she was hurt.

Examining her hands to assure herself that it was, indeed, but a dream, she observed their cleanliness with relief. She called back in the same tongue, assuring him of her safety.

Sinking back upon her sweat-ridden pillows, Verity sighed. Turning them over and punching them into submission, she worked out her frustration on being awakened so unexpectedly. This was not the first of her nightmares since they had moved to the island of Philae. Whether it was the rough transition, the loss of the familiar landscape she had enjoyed for the past decade, or the shocking circumstances surrounding the death of Linette, she could not tell. What she did know was that there was something about this place that was strange and wonderful all at once.

Housed within the walls of the temple, there was an oppressiveness that Verity had not felt in the desert. There, she could roam about the various dig sites and surrounding landscape with relative freedom. But here, the temple grounds were considered extremely fragile and warranted care even when walking through them. In addition, they were entirely surrounded by water, so if she had the desire to wander anywhere abroad, it meant the expense of a boat and a boatman, often along with the accompaniment of Lady Bethy, who insisted that it was unsafe for a young lady to travel about on her own in such a fashion. She felt tied to Philae every bit as much as though an invisible but taut and sinuous chain fastened her to it.

Although Verity was mightily grateful for Lady Bethy and

her generosity, she had begun to feel a sense of repression in her society. If Verity had not been so very much in her debt, she would often have escaped without her blessing, but, as it was, both the professor and Verity made sacrifices for the sake of the dig.

For it was all for the sake of the dig now. If Verity thought that the professor's obsession took precedence in their lives heretofore, she had vastly underrated his infatuation for his supposedly imminent and eminent discovery.

"Verity," he said one night as he prostrated himself across the floor, putting his eye up to a particularly quotidian-looking scrap of clay, "I do believe this – *this* could be it!"

Using his brushes and chisels, he chipped and swept away at the tiny scrap of dirt until nothing was left of it but crumbling sand.

The professor's temper had grown short in the sweltering Egyptian sun as the days went by with no further discoveries. It was particularly disturbing to him, as they had only a few short months in which to search, for the temples were due for their annual flooding in the midsummer months.

In one such fit of exasperation, he threw his chisel at the wall. It missed Verity's cheek by a hair's breadth, and she could hear the swish of the steel as it hurtled toward her. Striking the wall behind her, tears came unbidden to Verity as she watched the professor turn from her without a shred of regret or sorrow on his face. He immediately gave his complete attention to another piece of clay that surrounded him, along with papers, scrolls, and bits of pottery that were scattered across the floor.

Never a tender parent, the professor had at least always been mildly concerned with Verity's well-being and even had a habit of spoiling her with an impractical gift or two whenever he thought of it, which, indeed, was not very often.

However, such gifts were now nonexistent, as well as any shred of solicitude that he had ever shown his daughter. Nevertheless, she still attended to his needs unflinchingly, although with perhaps a little less tenderness than before.

Verity's mind retraced these thoughts until she realized that outside of her tent, more voices, louder even than before, seemed to be congregating. The language was hushed, but the murmurs sounded distressed.

Slipping her bare feet into a pair of sand-dusted, sturdy work boots near her bed, she grabbed a khaki tunic and wrapped it around her closely.

When she neared the flaps of her tent, she called out in Arabic, "Asim! Asim – is that you?"

"Yes, Miss Verity. I am here."

"What's going on out there?"

"To your bed. To your bed, you must go back," his words fell firm but gentle on the midnight air amongst the ever-growing din of voices.

"But Asim, what is going on out there?"

"It is not for your eyes, Miss Verity. To your bed."

"It is a sign of warning," said another man's voice.

Asim reprimanded him with a silencing hiss.

"It is Miss Verity. She has been awakened. We must not bring this worry to her door," he said in hushed tones to his comrade.

"It is already at her door!" was the disrespectfully toned response.

"Asim! I'm coming out."

"No, you must not, Miss Verity. It is not for your eyes," he repeated.

Verity attempted to open her tent flaps but struggled to do so as Asim seemed to be holding them shut.

"This must be cleared away first for you, Miss Verity."

"Asim – I want to help. I want to come out."

Verity watched the shadows dance before her against the front of her tent. She could just make out the outline of Asim - one hand raised up to grasp the folds of her tent.

There was a rush of movement as more men came to discover the source of the din. Asim was shoved aside. Verity seized her moment and ducked out from under the bottom of her tent flap. As she did so, she trod on something wet, spongy, and slippery. Springing away from it, she turned on her heel to face Asim.

As she looked down at her feet, her throat swelled up to emit another scream as she saw the raw flesh of a dead snake coiled around itself with its fangs encircling and pressing into its own tail.

Chapter Twenty-One

"I will not be deterred nor threatened!" exclaimed Lady Bethy to Professor Easton. "Nothing, no – *nothing* will keep us from this. That I promise you."

The professor nodded in agreement until his glasses slipped straight off of his nose to the very tip. Verity placed them back again in her usual dutiful manner. Lady Bethy threw her a glance of reprimand. She had been endeavoring to sever the professor's dependence on Verity to little avail.

"I *agree* with you, Lady Elizabeth. We are on form together upon that point, at least."

And, gathering the papers that he had laid out before him, he left the tent. It wasn't until he was long gone that Verity noticed that he'd somehow left a shoe behind under his chair.

Bending over to retrieve it, she was surprised by it

being knocked out of her hand by Lady Bethy's bejeweled walking stick, which that illustrious lady used on occasion.

"No, no, Verity. We have spoken about this. You are not to act as a slave to that man. He never rewards or even acknowledges you. It might have been considered sweet on very rare occasions when you were much younger, but now it looks ridiculous! I'll have my man attend to the shoe."

True to her word, she called to a servant outside, who deftly removed the shoe with much pomp and circumstance and, it is hoped, hastened it to its lopsided owner.

"Do you know," said Lady Bethy, fanning herself in the oppressive heat of the tent. "I rather fancied that I could be a marvelous stepmother to you at one point in time, but, and I speak this with no malice, your father is rather a bore. Not a bit of fun at all!"

To hear the word "father" often came as a shock to Verity's ears. It always took her a moment to connect the two images she had in her head of what a father should be and what, in actual fact, the professor was to her.

"Yes...I thought it would be amusing to be the wife of some great discoverer of ancient relics. I rather thought that Mr. Larcher would prove to be such, he took great interest in antiquities you know." Lady Bethy shrugged her shoulders with a great, slow sweep and a sigh, "But such is life. I simply can't seem to charm this father of yours. There is no accounting for taste, I suppose."

Verity laughed, "But you are married already, Lady

Bethy!"

"Am I? Oh, yes – I had nearly forgotten about my dear baronet! I have a letter from him somewhere."

Lady Bethy was quite as disorganized as the professor himself. Tufts of powder applicators, broken lipsticks, letters, hat pins, and more littered her vanity. She rummaged through it much as the professor had done amongst his papers. At last seizing upon an envelope with the seal still intact, she, after more riffling, found a sharp, silver letter opener and freed the missive.

"Yes, yes..." she said, scanning the page casually. "He still adores me. He's completed the transfer of funds into my Egyptian account. He wonders if he can join me? Hmm...I'll have to ferret out an excuse to prevent that. It would not do – it would not do at all to have him here."

Verity pondered to herself the intricacies of matrimony and was veritably confused by them.

She considered circumspectly before divulging her next thought, "I think he was – and still is – quite taken with my...my mother."

The appellation fell from Verity's lips gently and reverently as the first petal falls from a bloom that has been disturbed by the touch of a passerby.

Lady Bethy's head tipped to the side in perplexity: "My baronet is in love with your mother?"

"No, *no*, Lady Bethy. I meant the professor!"

The woman laughed at herself uproariously.

"Oh, of course. Of course you did, little dove," pausing to

tuck the missive into her bosom. "The Professor has made some fascinating discoveries of late, don't you think?" she continued, turning the conversation.

"Yes. He is particularly thrilled about that earring they identified. He believes it could lead to more discoveries soon. It's the right style of metalwork for the period."

"And he's been more amicable of late, as well, hasn't he?" Lady Bethy raised her heavy eyebrows in knowing inquiry.

"Indeed. It has been easier than usual to get on with him. He even gave me a small portion of money with which to treat myself the next time I take a boat across to town."

Verity blushed at the mention of money, mostly because she knew it really must have originated from Lady Bethy's aforementioned bank account but also because she was desperate to get to a proper town to do some shopping.

A few items from the magazines she so intensely poured over were rumored to have arrived in a market on the mainland. However, as Lady Bethy forbade her from going ashore alone, she was beholden to her caprice, and the two friends' desires did not always align.

"Are you terribly busy tomorrow?" Verity meekly inquired.

Lady Bethy, who was studying the effect of a new hairdo by holding bits of it up here and there, let it fall to her shoulders. Verity again noted the dark roots that tinged the red locks and puzzled why her friend would continue to color her hair so dramatically. Perhaps, however, that is why most men found her so fascinating.

"Little dove...all you think about is the new and the modern. Yes, I've seen your magazines," she said, arching a brow. "Does none of the ancient hold any interest for you?"

Shaking her head until a few strands of her own perfectly crimped hair fell amiss, Verity rejoined, "When you've been amongst it as much as I have, Lady Bethy, you wouldn't find it all so fascinating. It's been nothing but the ancient and decrepit ever since I was born. I want to see and feel and taste and touch only the new, new, *new*!"

"With the exception of a few scintillating baubles, eh?" Lady Bethy's words were muffled as she held a few hairpins between her teeth and continued work on her coiffure.

Turning toward the mirror, Verity could see her friend's reflection as Lady Bethy's eyes rested upon the ruby-encrusted lioness that was pinned upon her shoulder.

"Yes," Verity said, touching it fondly. "I *do* like this because *you* gave it to me."

"I'm glad, but you shouldn't set such store by baubles. It's not healthy!"

At this point, Lady Bethy let out a grumble of dissatisfaction and let her hair fall about her shoulders once again.

"I simply don't know how Linette did it so well. I feel like such an unprepossessing and absolute *blister*, as the baronet would say. Take pity on me, little dove, and help me with this tangled mess, will you?"

Verity's face had blanched at the mention of Linette. Although it had been many months since the tragic incident at the hotel, Verity still did not like to hear the maid's name mentioned.

Yet, dutiful as ever, she crossed over to her friend and, despite her shaking fingers, was able to coiffe Lady Bethy's hair perhaps even better than the Frenchwoman herself could have done.

"Thank you," said Lady Bethy as she patted and admired it appreciatively in the mirror.

For the first time looking at her friend's face, she said, "Oh, you don't still let *the incident* bother you, do you? It was probably some sex-crazed bounder who crashed the party. You must put it out of your mind if it disturbs you so."

Surprised at her friend's seemingly calloused attitude toward the still-painful subject, Verity rejoined, "I thought you told Major Nabil that you were convinced that it was a personal threat against you?"

"That was before I thought Mr. Rash…that is, I knew there was some opposition to my plans to move to Philae. What with the history supposedly connected to this place, it was incontrovertible in my mind that somebody was making a rather morbid gesture of warning."

Rather morbid? Verity was worried that her friend was sounding well-nigh flippant in her description of the horrifying event that had taken place.

When she looked up again, Verity could see that Lady Bethy was studying her intently in the mirror, a look of appraisal and a little contempt crossing her features for a moment.

The look vanished as soon as it was noted, and Lady Bethy arose, faced her friend, and enfolded her into a warm and lengthy embrace.

"*Of course* we shall go to town, little dove. But keep that money close. You may need every penny you can scrape together one day."

Verity wasn't certain, but was that a hint of a threat in Lady Bethy's usually kind and comforting voice?

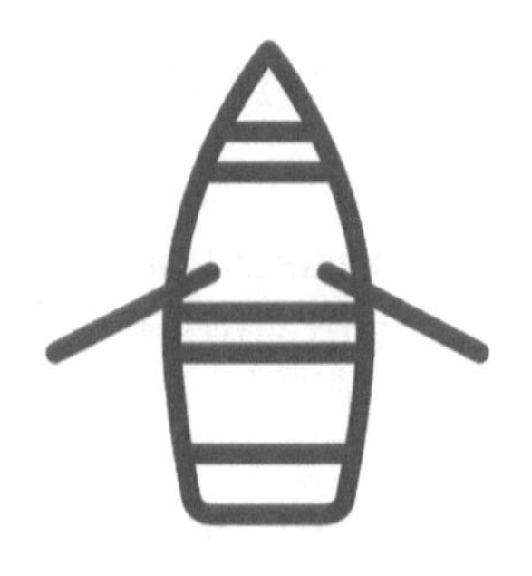

Chapter Twenty-Two

When Verity and Lady Bethy returned from their boat trip into town, Verity felt a heavy hand of disappointment on her heart. Under the watchful eye of her friend, she selected, then replaced, several items that had been the foremost desire of her mind for the past months.

The previous day's warning, combined with the disapproving glance of Lady Bethy, made Verity hesitant to spend the little money she had on such baubles. She, therefore, determined to try to escape at a later date in order to fetch the coveted goods. As she was busy mentally concocting a plan to do so, she noted that a strange boat was docked upon their return to Philae. What drew her interest particularly were the vibrant paintings on the side coupled with a fascinating name: Bisu. As she studied the beautiful lettering, her attention was arrested by a cacophony of shouts as their own watercraft scraped against the dock.

As the men moored their boat, Verity jumped lightly out of it, anxious for the professor's welfare. As she neared the encampment, one figure stood out amongst the rest of the milling mob of workers.

Ivory and gray robes swirled this way and that, dust was kicked up as men ran to and fro, hands were upraised in either excitement or terror – Verity could not tell which. Amongst it all, a stark figure in a black suit stood perfectly still. Not a breath of wind seemed to rustle his hair, nor a speck of dust touch the rich material of his ensemble.

Using a light scarf, Verity shielded the sand and sun from her face by wrapping it around her in the traditional fashion – a knack she had spent great pains to learn in honor of her mother. She approached the man, curious if he was a policeman or perhaps even the cause of this upheaval.

When she was just behind him, he suddenly whirled around.

It was Mr. Rashidi.

Apparently struck by her appearance, he took her hand and bent low over it. Then, he looked up into her face as she let the front of her scarf fall.

Dropping her hand, he staggered back a pace or two as though in astonishment.

"For a moment, Miss Verity, you resembled..."

Quick to recover himself, he straightened up once again to his full height. Looking haughty and not a bit ashamed of his former, near-subservient conduct, and with no further explanation, he politely inquired as to the nature of the whirlwind of bodies about them.

"I've simply no idea, Mr. Rashidi. We've only just arrived ourselves."

"We?" he probed.

"Yes, Lady Bethy and myself."

Glancing over Verity's shoulder, Mr. Rashidi acknowledged the presence of her illustrious companion with a curt nod.

Verity puzzled within herself at the almost intangible shift that had taken place in their relationship ever since the party whereat they had lost poor Linette.

Lady Bethy used to comport herself toward him very much as she did any other man – flirting, teasing, and even relying on him when her former lover cornered and abused her. And Mr. Rashidi had paid her in kind – accepting her little attentions and giving back compliments as soon as she hinted at them, as most attractive women who are accustomed to attention are wont to do.

As the two greeted each other more formally, there was a steeliness between them, as though they both held either end of an unbreakable twine and were forever silently and desperately attempting to pull it toward their own favor.

Each was unflinching.

"Is this hullabaloo down to you, then, Mr. Rashidi?" erupted Lady Bethy as soon as she was near enough for them to hear her above the din. "My bird is very distressed at all this racket. I shall hold you responsible if he begins to molt!"

This was said in a half-serious, half-flirtatious tone, accompanied by an arched brow and a rather excessive batting of darkened and falsely elongated lashes. Verity could tell that the smile that revealed her friend's glittering teeth was all but welcoming.

"I would expect that it was much more likely down to *you*, Lady Elizabeth," he bowed with much grace, attempting to repay her coquetry, but venom was thick in his voice. "You make a stir wherever you go."

"Blow the man down!" chimed in Bartholomew, cleverly sensing his mistress's true sentiments.

Feeling awkward in such a tense atmosphere, Verity ventured to extricate herself by cutting into it with a soft, "I must go and see if the Professor needs me."

"Not a bit of it, my girl," said Lady Bethy in a booming, draconian voice.

After registering the surprise in Mr. Rashidi's face, she softened her tone, "We'll go together, little dove, for we both must know what has come to pass."

"I shall accompany you," Mr. Rashidi broke in firmly.

Lady Bethy's face seemed to have nearly turned to stone as her usual smiles melted away. Perhaps unable to think of a legitimate excuse for him not to do so, she sailed past him with a determined step.

Taking the lead, Verity practically had to shove her way

through the crowd, but as she neared the center of it, words and phrases came to her that gave her already tremulant heart even more cause to beat rapidly.

Far ahead of her companions, she at last reached the tent of the professor. From what the men around her were shouting, she expected to see him surrounded by a swarm of chattering people.

Instead, he was alone, slumped over in his chair, something grasped tightly in his pale hand.

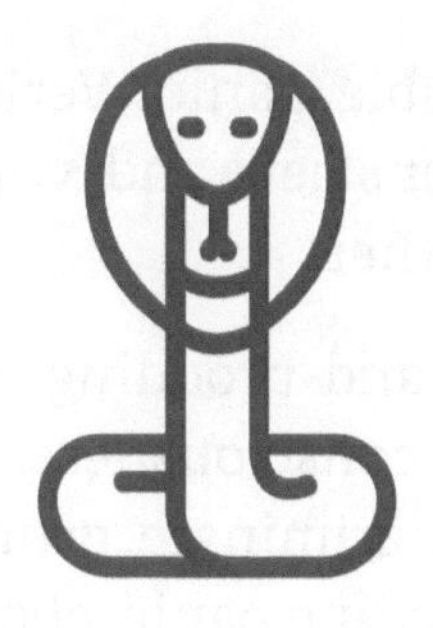

Chapter Twenty-Three

For a moment, Verity was convinced he was dead. Trembling, she reached a hand up to his forehead and brushed the tangled mess of gray locks back from his brow. Was his skin warm to the touch? Would it be cold in this heat if he was dead? The hair promptly fell back against his forehead, but then it fluttered straight up again, not by Verity's touch but by his sleeping breath.

A little movement of his chest, a slight snore, and Verity let out a sigh that was a mixture of exasperation and relief. She reached down to his hand to gently shake him, and as she did so, his hand unfurled, revealing a golden serpent figurine. Taking it from him, she moved it back and forth as it glinted in the thin strip of light that poured in from a gap in the tent. The blue eyes of the snake were surely sapphires, so deep and lustrous was their sheen. They seemed to glimmer with the fire of the most calescent flame.

Just then, Lady Bethy and Mr. Rashidi entered the

tent. With inexplicable panic, Verity hid her precious discovery prize up her sleeve and, with great earnestness, began to wake her father.

With much poking and prodding, he, at last, came to some semblance of consciousness. Hazily greeting his guests with an indiscriminate grunt or two, he began looking, with heightening panic, about his person.

"Where is the damned thing? I had it here just a moment ago! And Lady Bethy - she will assuredly need to see it, to prove –"

"What is it, Professor? For what are you seeking?" chimed in Mr. Rashidi.

"It's a snake! *The* snake, of course!" exclaimed the professor.

Lady Bethy lifted up her skirts in alarm, disturbing her bird as she did so.

"Snakes? Where?" she cried out with a slightly strangled voice. "I can't abide the creatures!"

"Then you have ventured to the wrong country, Lady Elizabeth," came the wry rejoinder from Mr. Rashidi.

Giving him a disdainful glance in return for his veiled remark, she continued to look about her feet as she performed a sort of ungainly dance, most likely in the hope that she could stamp upon the head of a snake if it had the audacity to venture a nip at her ankles.

Mr. Rashidi grabbed a nearby stick and used it to cautiously lift up the blankets on the cot.

Bartholomew added to the bedlam by circling the

room, mimicking his mistress with, "The creatures! The creeeeeatures!"

Verity, knowing full well that her father meant the mysterious curio hidden in her sleeve, feigned to join the group as they poked about the corners, looking for his treasured trinket or venomous vermin, depending on the point of view of each companion.

Although Verity often tried to tidy the professor's room, he somehow was able to make it look as though it had been ransacked by a thief whenever he returned to it. Papers and tools were littered about the sandy stone floor, and it smelled strangely of mothballs, although Verity knew he never used them to store his clothes.

The professor, meanwhile, was mumbling under his breath, "The sapphires alone must prove its origins and worth. It is priceless...*priceless*!"

"Did you say 'sapphires,' Professor?" queried Lady Bethy, letting her skirts drop at the mention of the jewels.

"Yes, of course, sapphires. They are unquestionably not made of glass. I've never seen such fine specimens in all my life, and that's saying something."

The last was addressed more to himself than to the surrounding company.

"Professor..." continued Lady Bethy, "Do you mean to say that this serpent you speak of is made of...of precious jewels?"

"Why, of course. You trust me to know the difference, don't you? I've been looking for it for ten years!"

"So it is not a *live* snake?" queried Mr. Rashidi.

The professor harrumphed, "Of course not."

Just then, Bartholomew landed on Verity's arm, sinking his talons uncomfortably into her sleeve – and a little into her flesh – to steady himself. He began pecking at her arm, just where she had hidden the snake.

The pain of his relentless actions caused Verity to shake herself from her heretofore selfish concealment. Why was she hiding it? It was silly to believe that she wouldn't be found out sooner or later. What had compelled her to do so in the first place?

Shaking off the troublesome macaw, Verity stooped behind the professor's armchair.

She feigned an expression of surprise as she slipped the ornament out of her sleeve and called out, "I think I've found it!"

When she elevated herself, she could see Mr. Rashidi looking at her appraisingly. Feeling her cheeks fill with the heat of discomfiture, she quickly placed the snake into the sweaty palm of the eager professor.

"You see? The finest sapphires, and the snake surely is pure gold – not merely gilded – and it would fit in fine and perfect form, wouldn't you agree?"

He held the snake up to the hungry eyes of Lady Bethy and Mr. Rashidi, whose faces nearly touched, cheek to cheek, as they drew together for a closer inspection.

"Fit on what?" exclaimed Lady Bethy.

"What is it?" sounded out Mr. Rashidi simultaneously.

"Why, don't you know? Can't you tell?" the professor asked, astonished at their ignorance.

They shook their heads in unison.

Triumphantly, the professor declared, "It is the uraeus from the headdress of Queen Nefertiti herself!"

Chapter Twenty-Four

Four individuals crowded close to the round table in the center of the artifact room. Little exclamations of excitement escaped each in turn as they poured over the newspaper before them.

Verity, the professor, Lady Bethy, and Mr. Rashidi all began speaking at once in reference to the article in the London Times about the professor's discovery. As an ardent reader of magazines, Verity was thrilled to the tips of her fingers as she traced her own image printed in black and white.

In order to display the uraeus properly, the professor and Lady Bethy had commissioned a replica of a cap crown. Studying photographs of Thutmoses' bust of Nefertiti that was housed in Germany, the two of them overinstructed and cajoled a poor tradesman to the absolute edge of his patience as he fashioned it. Despite their haranguing, however, the artisan had managed to make a striking resemblance to the crown of the ancient

Egyptian queen. The effect was magnificent – especially the way he had fashioned the two intertwining striped ribbons that were held fast by a golden diadem upon which the snake figurine was attached.

There had been a great controversy as to whom should model the crown for the photograph. First, Lady Bethy insisted that she wear it, claiming it as her right in return for funding the dig. Verity wholeheartedly agreed that her friend would look magnificent with the crown placed upon her flaming russet hair.

Mr. Rashidi had strongly objected, contending that the British protectorate ended in 1922 and that she had no right as a British peeress to exert her power in such a way. Instead, he insisted that a local woman of the same age and feature as the bust be used.

Flinging daggers of insults back and forth until it made Verity's head split, she attempted to soothe them into some semblance of conciliation. Her gentle words at first fell silent upon the heavy air. But in that moment, they both looked upon her as though a shaft of light had entered both of their minds at once.

"She's perfect!" Lady Bethy exclaimed, taking Verity by the arm and forcing her to turn in a full circle.

"I agree with you, Lady Elizabeth. It would solve both of our issues happily," agreed Mr. Rashidi as he stared into Verity's face appraisingly.

Feeling flustered at this sudden attention upon her person, Verity disengaged herself from her friend's grasp.

"What are you talking about?" Verity inquired nervously.

"You! It's simply destiny, my dear. *You* shall wear the headdress for the photograph! You're Egyptian *and* British…" gushed Lady Bethy.

"You know the customs and culture of this, your mother's home country, better now than when we first met a decade ago," continued Mr. Rashidi.

"You'll look glorious with it. We'll design a gown to match," raved Lady Bethy.

"It is a most advantageous solution," bowed Mr. Rashidi.

They both looked to the professor as though seeking his opinion and permission, but he had already turned away and was feverishly writing some letter or other. Verity thought it was quite probably a virulent response to a congratulatory epistle from one of his former colleagues. She had penned many such a missive for him in recent days.

As Lady Bethy's plans unfolded, Verity became absolutely enchanted by the idea of playing Queen Nefertiti. Never a forward – and often, a neglected – girl, she relished the idea of commanding respect and attention with clothes and jewels she had long coveted.

It was settled. In preparation, the two women made an appointment with an illustrious clothing designer in Aswan. Upon arrival, Verity sat in awe of Madame Adelaide. The seamstress sat as straight as a statue and looked over her darkened spectacles that were perched at the end of her long, thin nose. Each time she appraised Verity's figure, her nose wrinkled as though she was sniffing something unpleasant. Knowing her plain garb was nothing compared to Lady Bethy's, nor the models' and assistants' neat uniforms that milled around them, Verity was supremely uncomfortable. Especially as she gazed enviously at Madame Adelaide's sharply-cut, western-style suit that fit her bony figure flawlessly.

After many sketches and several models were presented to them, a gown was at last selected to be the base of the costume. Long, ivory pleats of gentle gauze rippled over the model's legs as she walked to and fro upon the velvet carpet. Verity longed to feel the swish of the material brush against her own legs and closed her eyes, imagining it.

She envisioned herself reclining upon a stone-framed bed, the middle of which was strung with intricately woven reeds that bowed comfortably as her weight pressed into them. A bowl of ripe figs, their purple flesh carved open to reveal scrumptiously pink inflorescence, were drizzled with sticky honey.

She reached for one and was about to place it upon her lips when Lady Bethy exclaimed, "What on the gods' earth are you doing, Verity?"

Verity's eyes fluttered open to perceive that she held a Cuban-heeled shoe inches from her mouth. The heat of the room had been so oppressive, she had fallen asleep and slipped into a near-waking dream.

Setting aside the shoe with as much decorum as she could muster, she mumbled an apology and strained her eyes to open fully until they watered with the effort.

"Do you think you could peel yourself away from the footwear long enough to be measured for your gown, little dove?" Lady Bethy's voice, despite the tender appellation, was quite stern.

Verity nodded and stood, then was directed to a back room where the selected dress was placed upon her deftly by Madame Adelaide's capable assistants. It resembled the kalasiris of the ancient times – a form-fitting sheath with straps that crossed and attached at the back of her neck. The ivory linen was so fine, it hugged her form, and the pleats caressed her skin sumptuously.

So enraptured was she with the feel of such elegant material, she hardly remembered to be embarrassed as Madame Adelaide and Lady Bethy poked and prodded at her, discussing the alterations that were necessary for the costume.

The outcome was truly transformative. Less than a week later, when the photographer from the newspaper was scheduled to travel out to the dig site, Verity again relished the feeling of the cool fabric upon her skin. She admired how Madame Adelaide's skill accentuated her modest form in a way that made her look older...regal, even. Drawing herself up to her full height, she had but a moment to examine herself before Lady Bethy hallooed her way in, accompanied by a short gentleman who looked rather sweaty and distressed.

It turned out to be a theatrical man who had been cajoled into traveling to their encampment. He had just come from a matinee performance, and the makeup still lay thick upon his face. He was to assist Verity with the application of grease paint to complete her metamorphosis into the ancient queen.

As the man began to cover her face with the paint, they came almost nose to nose. It took all of Verity's fortitude not to laugh at the artist's funny pink cheeks and darkened mustachios, evidence left over from his performance only hours before.

As he began to make the application around her eyes, she lowered her lids to accommodate him, and her gaze could not be moved from his upper lip. As his tongue darted out from between his teeth this way and that in concentration, she nearly lost her presence of mind and laughed out loud – particularly when the wetness of his tongue began to interfere with the blackness of the aforementioned mustaches and dripped paint down his shirtfront. After an anguishing hour of repressed hilarity, Verity was at last ready for the photograph.

Standing perfectly still and trying with all her might to exude feminine power, the image was soon set for all time within the strange black-and-silver box into which she peered as the bright light flashed, for Verity had never before had her photograph captured.

Now, as she looked at the result, she was proud of her heritage and felt a connection to her mother as never before. She looked quite grown up – a fact that had crept up on her without her taking notice until that moment when she stared down at the reflected image of herself as she and her three companions studied it around that table. Yes – she was a woman now. There was no denying it any longer, no matter how often the professor treated her as a child or how much Lady Bethy kept a watchful eye upon her.

Lost in a world of her own, Verity could hardly hear Mr. Rashidi and the professor arguing about what should now be done with the artifact.

"It should be displayed in the Egyptian Museum in Cairo! You have no right to take it from my country!" Mr. Rashidi argued convincingly.

The professor, his loyalty no longer attached to the British Museum, as his funding from that eminent institution had ceased, said dreamily, "Wouldn't it be marvelous if it could be encased alongside Thutmose's bust? That way, they could be studied together. People would come from all over the world to witness them side by side."

Lady Bethy's decisive voice cut across the dispute: "It shall remain with me until further notice. It is *my* money that has provided the means of this discovery. Therefore, unless legal action is taken by the Egyptian Kingdom, Mr. Rashidi, or until you find some better reason for it to leave my side than sitting in a dusty museum, Professor Easton, it shall be under *my* protection."

As neither man had the courage to thwart her in that moment, she defiantly placed the uraeus inside its small, velvet-lined box.

Tucking it under her arm with resolution, she swept out of the tent and into the night, her scarlet macaw hovering behind her and squawking in agreement: "My protection. My protection!"

Chapter Twenty-Five

Verity was awakened by a cold hand resting on her arm. With a sharp intake of breath, she opened her eyes to behold a small child. The girl was barefoot and wearing only a loose nightdress. Verity, concerned about the child's welfare, sat up, removed the blanket at her feet, and offered it to the girl.

The waif merely shook her short locks and offered Verity a half-smile, tilting her head to the side as she did so.

"Where did you come from, little one? Have you lost your father?"

The only response Verity received in return was another shake of the dark hair.

Verity could only believe that one of the workers had sneaked his child into the encampment – a practice strictly forbidden as the environment could prove dangerous. She had compassion on the child and did not wish to get her father into trouble.

"I won't tell," she continued comfortingly. "Let's just get you back to your bed so you're safe and warm."

In reply, the child pressed her finger to her lips and beckoned Verity toward the front of the tent.

Quicker than expected, the girl scampered out into the night before Verity had time to fetch a shawl or shoes. Without thinking, she dashed after the little thing in form and fashion with nothing but her nightgown to warm her.

Darting this way and that, Verity had difficulty keeping up with the girl as they ventured through the temple. Whenever she believed the white figure was lost to her, the girl's heart-shaped face would appear around a column or a tower of boxes, smiling mischievously and summoning Verity toward her once again.

Longing to find out more about her mysterious guide, Verity made plans to note the tent to which she led her and resolved that on the morrow, she would privately inquire into her circumstances. Perhaps Verity could be of use to the family in some way. A man who was desperate enough to bring a child into such perilous circumstances might be a widower with other children to provide for as well.

As they crept through the canvas and ropes, the chill of the desert air made Verity at first regret the chase. However, the little scamp was so agile, Verity quickly warmed and almost began to enjoy their strange adventure together. Never before had she hazarded a walk in the middle of the night through the encampment. Verity greatly valued her sleep, so the thought had never occurred to her.

It was a disparate scene under the silvery moon. The shade that provided a welcome respite from the heat of the day now transcended into haunting shadows from the great walls and columns that stretched toward the stars. The scents were different, too. Gone was the stench of sweaty men working in the hot sun. No more could she smell the unsettled dust that tickled her nose as the men moved mounds of earth. Instead, the water that surrounded the temple filled the air with a strange crispness that made her expand her chest until she was almost dizzy with the effort.

Without warning, the girl stopped outside of a large pavilion. Busy enjoying the metamorphic sights and sounds in her eager and sleep-deprived mind, Verity altogether forgot to note the last few twists and turns the child had taken.

Unfastening and hoisting up the heavy flap at the entrance, the girl made a signal for Verity to enter. As the child did so, Verity's eyes adjusted from the tenebrous night to the little flames that had been lit at the entrance.

It was not a workman's simple tent. This one was lavishly furnished with all the comforts that Europe and Egypt had to offer.

This was unmistakeably Lady Bethy's quarters.

The child took Verity's hand and led her deeper into the belly of the structure until they were just outside a strip of hanging curtains where Verity knew Lady Bethy must be sleeping.

Upon a perch in his cage sat Lady Bethy's parrot, ostensibly lost in slumber. Verity wondered why his cage had not been covered for the night as was usual.

Kneeling before an enormous trunk, the child intimated that Verity should join her. Obediently, Verity fell softly to her knees but then shook her head at the girl. With an almost wicked smile that transformed her features from innocence to impishness, the girl deftly picked the lock, lifted the lid, and began rummaging in the mess of objects that appeared before them both. Verty's stomach dropped in fear as swiftly as the lock fell from its latch.

"No," Verity whispered in tones kind yet firm, "We mustn't be here. These are Lady Bethy's things."

Ignoring her susurrations, the child continued to pillage gleefully until she removed something Verity recognized: the box that encased the coveted serpent.

Verity tried to pull the girl away, but the little thing's thin arms belied their strength, and she easily broke free. Opening the case eagerly, the child removed the uraeus and, holding it up to the meager light, turned it this way and that, admiring the sapphires with a seemingly experienced eye.

Then, in an inexplicable act of generosity, the child held it out in her palm and gesticulated to Verity that she should take it. Shaking her head, Verity took up the box and, through a series of further gestures, tried to intimate that they return the precious object to its former resting place.

The girl rolled her eyes and shrugged her shoulders. Then, with a wicked grin, she looked Verity steadily in the eye as she closed her fingers one by one over the priceless ornament and stood up. As her eyes darted toward the doorway of the tent, Verity realized her intention and stood also, resolving to prevent the theft.

As she lunged toward the little mite, she second-guessed her violence upon so small a person at the last moment, misjudged her footing, twirled around in a sort of pirouette, and landed hard, her head striking against the edge of the trunk. The last thing her eyes could discern before becoming unfocused was the devilish grin of the girl as she turned back before absconding into the night with panther-like movements.

Verity felt blood trickle down the back of her head, and just as she was about to lose consciousness, Bartholomew startled her with a great, "Sound the alarm! Sound the alarm!" in his gratingly sing-song voice.

Before Verity could gather her wits, Lady Bethy's voice bellowed, "What on the gods' earth *are* you doing here, Verity?"

Chapter Twenty-Six

Verity scrambled to her knees but felt dizzy while completing the action and could not move to bring herself to her feet. She glanced up at Lady Bethy, who looked as though she had been poured into the yellow, silken, floor-length negligee as it showed off nearly every inch of her form. The only aspect that remained a mystery was her ankles, where the nightgown flared out fashionably.

It was at the base of this lustrous hem that Verity found herself staring at incomprehensibly. Knowing full well how strange her position must look and at a loss as to what to say or do, she merely remained kneeling – perfectly still, waiting for whatever must ensue.

Should she pretend that she had been sleepwalking and had an accident while unconscious of her movements? Could she feign a fainting fit? Would Lady Bethy believe her if she simply told the truth of the child's actions? Frozen in a fog of indecisiveness and pain, she chose to do nothing.

"What are you doing here, Verity?" repeated Lady Bethy more firmly.

Her tone was stern, but what hurt Verity the most was the absence of that much-treasured epithet "little dove." Verity could not even look up to meet her eye.

Reaching down, Lady Bethy removed the box from Verity's clammy grasp. She must have noted the missing contents, of course, for the box came to a clattering drop just before Verity's face.

Hardly blinking at the near miss, she next felt hot hands encircling her upper arms as she was helped forcibly to her feet. Still unable to meet the eye of her friend, Verity stood there, mute and shivering.

Whether pity overtook the older woman's heart, Verity did not know, but a shawl was placed upon her shoulders. She could hear her friend calling to someone but could not make out what she was saying. It was as though someone had placed a feathered pillow over her ears, so strange came the muted sounds to her. Soon, Verity was accompanied, stumblingly, through the intricate network of the camp until she was thrust back into her own modestly furnished tent by persons unseen and unknown.

Collapsing upon her bed, a whirlwind of emotion was released onto her pillow. Never has a daughter sobbed more earnestly for her mother than Verity did for the certainty that she had lost the love and respect of the only maternal figure she had ever known.

The entire situation felt like a horrid nightmare from which she could not awaken, but what could she do? She could not prove her innocence. The thought of blaming a child made her feel ill – and if the child or the treasure could not be recovered, she would be in an even worse position in the sight of her friend.

Finally falling asleep, she had fitful nightmares that made her sob and shiver as the night wore into day. Still sleeping and dreaming, a fever erupted somewhere amongst her visions.

Throughout the subsequent days, Verity drifted in and out of consciousness. The delirium that overtook her was wholly consuming. She could never be sure of what was reality and what was part of the fantasy dream world that was becoming more real to her every day.

Haunted by the child, visions of the young imp incessantly materialized before her. The girl became almost a spiritual guide, leading her into the reoccurring dream of her childhood. These fantasies had all but ceased once she had settled into her life at the camp near Aswan, but since Lady Bethy's dinner party at the Old Cataract Hotel where poor Linette had been murdered, they had returned to Verity with abundant force.

She did not know how many days had passed since that fateful night of the stolen trinket. But one night, when Verity had been tossing and twisting in her sweltering sheets in a fit of fever, the girl materialized as though from the particles of desert sand that covered the floor at the foot of her bed.

Sighing with an odd sense of contentment, she followed

the girl willingly. It was not through the pillars of Philae under which she walked, however, but through a resplendent palace. Gliding past wide columns thick with paints of every color imaginable, she looked down at her feet and admired the peaked toes of her intricately wrought, gilded papyrus leaf sandals. Her diaphanous sheath dress was cinched with a rufescent sash around her waist and swished to and fro in tandem with the swing of her hips as she stepped through to an inner courtyard.

Sitting by the pool that was the centerpiece of the enclosure, she bent down to admire her appearance. The banded collar at her neck was fashioned with plates of pure gold interlaid with carnelian. The effect of the ensemble was entrancing. Not a hair was out of place in her carefully braided wig that was bedecked at the tips with beads. They clinked and tinkled together as a few fell into her face, and she shook them back luxuriantly.

A sleek, well-kempt cat scampered past her, and she watched it intently as its haunches grew tense when poised to ascend a staircase in pursuit of some unseen prey.

Following the feline, she, too, mounted the steep steps to the upper floor. Looking out upon the vista that appeared before her, she felt supreme contentment in the knowledge that all she could see was her own – her very own to relish and make as she desired, guided by her slightest whim.

Just as she was about to turn her back to the bewitching scene, she heard voices beneath her. Peering over the wall, she noted two workmen who were repairing a weakness in the structure. Both were busily engaged – one calmly and methodically, while the other was flourishing his trowel about lustily.

Verity smiled to herself at the contrast between the two and moved toward them for a closer examination of the quality of their work. Calling out to them, she saw that her presence startled the more meticulous of the two. He veritably shook the precarious scaffolding as he dropped his tools and genuflected immediately at her presence. This caused the other to brandish his utensil with even more abandon, and a splatter of mud struck Verity across her face and neck. Glancing down at her bejeweled bosom, she haughtily observed the straw-littered mud that defiled her exquisite adornments.

A strange, blazing rage overtook her as though a fiery current of lightning struck her mind, and she heard words of asperity pour out of her: "Ahmaq – fool! Look what you have done!"

The man, observing her appearance for the first time, gave her a moderate bow but leered up at her as he did so. Then, taking a nearby rope that was loosely hanging from where it was secured at a rampart near her, he clambered up effortlessly until he could see over the top of the wall.

"I do look upon you," he said, his eyes following the entire length of her form lecherously. "And it is great beauty that I behold."

With some hitherto unexposed womanly intuition, Verity traced the outline of her thigh sensually, lifting her skirt as she did so. The man was entranced by her action until, from a hidden sheath wrapped around her leg, she seized a sharpened, curved dagger.

He must not have seen it, for when she moved closer to him, he made as though to continue his pursuit of her over the parapet, but she was as quick and stealthy as the cat she had followed only moments before.

Before his leg could ascend the rampart, she had the knife at his throat.

"You dare – you dare to molest *me*?"

The man made no answer but for a laugh that bespoke his apparent bemusement at her attempt at violence.

With the full force of her form, she pushed him over the wall. His hand slipped, and he was just able to twist the rope around his hand to save himself from a fall that would have surely meant death from that height.

Fear only began to manifest upon his visage when he saw what she had begun to do. Taking the knife, she slowly commenced cutting through tendril after tendril of the rope.

Desperately, he tried to mount the wall, but he would never make it in time.

"Musaeida!" he called out for help to the other workman, who was still prostrated and now trembling.

Gazing up at her, the offending workman's next words rang out clear and urgent.

"Please," he pleaded. "Please. Do not do this thing."

The voice awakened her from the dream.

A very real knife was in Verity's hand, and she was

staring down into the terrified features of an entirely different man than the one who looked up at her in her dream. An expression of desperate pleading was the only resemblance the two men shared.

Without thought, Verity pressed the knife hard into the last thread of rope that lay against the stone. No outcry escaped the man's lips as she watched his face disappear into the shadowy chasm below.

Chapter Twenty-Seven

Trembling, Verity heard the knife clatter against the outer rim of the shaft and watched it fall with a dull thud to the ground beside her. It was no glittering, gilded knife akin to the one in her dream, but instead, it was crafted from ordinary tapered steel and splintery wood. One such splinter had caught in her palm, and it cut farther into her flesh as she wrung her hands in anguish.

She was standing, not before the ramparts of an imposing palace but near the shaft in which Nefertiti's headdress piece had been unearthed. It was fathoms deep, and Verity was certain there was no chance of the man's survival.

The body would surely be discovered in the morning, and Verity had little time to work out what to do. The first thing was to rid herself of the knife. The most logical place was the shaft itself, so she threw it down after the man. Perhaps they would somehow believe that it was an accident or even that the man had meant to do away with himself.

Stumbling back to her tent, she sat down upon a chair. It was nearly dawn, and she felt sure that someone would come to wake her soon. Using the washbasin to cleanse her dusty feet, she soon realized that it was silly to have washed them so far from her bed. The water splashed to the floor in evidence, and her feet would become covered with dust again as soon as they stepped on the ground.

Thinking quickly, she stretched her toes out onto her vanity and, balancing gingerly, reached down to gather up handfuls of dust and sand, scattering them until the droplets of liquid were indistinguishable. Next, she adjusted carefully on her chair, measured the distance with a keen eye, and leaped across to her bed, despite her trembling legs.

Breathless in her efforts, she enfolded herself within her thin blanket and waited there, shivering with her wet feet, until she heard footsteps. Someone had entered her tent, but her mind was so awhirl with what had come to pass that she did not have the capacity to even wonder who it could be.

The person moved toward her, stopping near her vanity table. Wooden legs scraped against the floor as the individual dragged a chair toward her bedside. It creaked as the weight of the person sat beside her.

"Where is it?" a low voice hissed. "Where is it, young Verity?"

The spindly legs of the chair crepitated again as the unknown personage shifted their weight.

"I have searched every inch of this room while you've been in a delirium. I need you to awaken now and tell me where it is!"

Sounding more familiar as it continued to speak, the voice made a groan. Verity, at last swimming to the surface of her stupor, moved ever so slightly in her bed, so she could see her visitor.

Black material was barely distinguishable from the dusky ambiance of the room, but Verity could just make out a pair of trousered legs. With her movement, the man had fallen silent and held as perfectly still as Verity.

It felt as though years stretched out between them in this silent battle of self-control. Verity wanted nothing more than to throw back the covers and scream until someone came to her rescue or to his. For the realization came upon her that she could be as much of a danger to him as she now felt his presence threatened her.

Just as Verity felt she couldn't stand the apprehension any longer, both of them flinched as a muffled voice fell upon their ears from outside the tent.

Gradually, slowly, the figure stood up and moved toward the exit. As he pulled back the flap of the tent, Verity threw caution to the wind and sat up in bed. The movement caught the attention of the interloper, and he turned back and locked eyes with Verity, the first blush of the aurora streaming upon his face.

It was Mr. Rashidi.

He said no word of acknowledgment but merely let the material fall as a separation between them.

Verity was aghast with this intrusion. Did he know of her evil deed? Had he witnessed it? What on earth was he doing at the encampment at that time of the morning? And did he say that he had searched her premises before? She was frightened. Determined to seek the help of Lady Bethy immediately, she began to dress herself after gingerly wrapping her splintered palm.

In the midst of her preparations, she sullenly sat down upon her bed. Lady Bethy would most likely, under the circumstances, have no desire to see or even speak to her unless it was to interrogate her about the theft of the snake.

Her father was, therefore, her only hope for sympathy and action on this occasion. She could at least complain of Mr. Rashidi's behavior and beg some protection from the man, whether or not he knew of her inexplicable and lamentable actions. Resuming her preparations, she was surprised by her weakness, having no knowledge of her prolonged unconsciousness.

When she put on a dress that usually fit her well, she noticed that it hung loosely on her frame. Upon sitting down at her vanity mirror, she noted both hollow cheek and sunken eye that gave her some elucidation as to her recent welfare. She realized that her fitful sleep was not that of one night but was the result of some illness of extended duration.

This revelation brought her comfort in light of her recent actions. Perhaps, if the truth of her guilt was exposed, she could make a plea of madness brought on by this inexplicable infirmity.

After finishing her preparations, with feeble knees and shuffling feet, Verity made her way to her father's tent.

Chapter Twenty-Eight

Lady Bethy's voluptuous figure was the first that greeted her as she walked through to her father's chambers. The two women stared at each other for a moment, the striking contrast between them more discernible than ever. The peeress had a healthy glow to her cheeks that were pronounced the more, along with her full lips, by her well-cut, deep magenta dress; the younger woman, in her simple, belted, khaki frock made her bones seem to jut out at unusual and uncomfortable angles.

The violated eagerness that had propelled Verity toward her father's presence was drained from her as quickly and forcefully as Lady Bethy was sucking a Shamouti orange.

What happened next shocked Verity to her core.

Moving rapidly to her side, Lady Bethy raised her hand to Verity's face. Expecting a slap, Verity braced herself for what she considered to be well-deserved violence. Instead, Lady Bethy took Verity's cheek in her hand and caressed it with all the care of a tender parent.

Rather than upbraid Verity for her recreant behavior, Lady Bethy tossed aside the orange she had sucked dry and said, "You have come back to us at last."

She then folded the young woman into a benevolent embrace until Verity's knees gave out, and she melted into oblivion.

When she awoke, the professor's face came hazily into view as though he was shrouded in a wreath of clouds. Behind him, she could barely discern Lady Bethy, who was speaking to a man with spectacles who wore an unusually dusty, cream-colored jacket. Bartholomew was on the floor, tearing at the remains of the orange, nibbling at its decimated contents. On either side of her, servants she recognized as those of Lady Bethy were fanning Verity assiduously. As her eyes focused, one of them tried to press a glass of cool water to her lips. She partook with gusto.

"What is your thought, Doctor?" she could hear Lady Bethy inquire. "Is she out of danger?"

"Yes, I believe so. The fever has gone absolutely. She is just a little frail at present. Let her rest as much as possible. I cannot think what gave her the strength or inclination to walk this far."

"And what may we feed her?" continued the peeress inquiringly.

The doctor began to rattle off a list of bland and easily palatable foods while Verity's attention focused on the Professor.

For the first time in Verity's life, she could see concern cross his features as he looked into her face. Usually, the only look she garnered from him was mild surprise after having forgotten her presence, but this expression of faint solicitousness was novel, and – dare she let herself feel it? Gratifying.

Longing to continue tracing the effect of the heretofore unknown emotion on his face, she sadly could not find the strength to do so and instead shut her eyelids slowly. In a strange half-consciousness, she could still hear the voices around her. Smiling contentedly to herself, she was arrested from her pleasurable state by the voice of Mr. Rashidi.

"I heard the doctor was attending here. Please come quickly – an accident has taken place."

The two Egyptian men rushed from the room, speaking Arabic in anxious tones.

It was as though an arrow had pierced Verity's heart. The peaceful rest was quiveringly dispelled as she realized the reason for Mr. Rashidi's urgency. A flood of terror washed over her, but she knew she must act in haste. Steeling herself against what might come, she opened her eyes and lifted herself onto one of her forearms to a semi-recumbent pose.

"F...Father," Verity spoke the title with great timidity, hoping that the purportedly tender appellation would awaken his senses to a protective state when she delivered her account.

The professor responded by sending his glasses flying in

alarm.

"Verity? Are you quite alright, my child? Only you've never..." he trailed off, blinking rather blankly into her face.

"Yes, Father," she said, pressing on despite his marginally adverse reaction to the designation. "I...I have something to tell you."

"What is it, Verity?"

A shaft of light from the uplifted tent flap shone in upon her pathetic state. He looked at her with the utmost tenderness and concern. She had never before felt completely in command of his attention until that moment. Verity determined to make the most of it.

"Mr. Rashidi came to my room early this morning – alone," she reported in a dry, mechanical voice.

"Oh, my dear daughter. Did he...did he...*interfere* with you in any way?" the professor twisted his mouth as though the words tasted sour as they fell from his lips.

"No, Profe – Father," she corrected herself, unwilling to lose the tender care that this sacred name had begun to elicit. "I am quite safe, and...and...*whole*, but still – he should not have done it, should he?"

Her eyes pleaded with him in supplication, craving to convey the innocence that he always assumed in her.

"No, child, he should not have done it," the professor agreed with a crooked, disdainful smile.

It was then that Lady Bethy stepped in, brandishing a hand and sweeping away the freshly tender parent.

"I've had a feeling that man was up to no good ever since he came, uninvited and unannounced. What *is* he doing here? What right has he to put his nose in where it isn't wanted? We will have him banished from the site immediately."

Breathing just a little more freely, Verity felt grateful for Lady Bethy's protective spirit, albeit in other circumstances, it could feel domineering – even smothering. She was a woman who liked her own way in all things.

"You know perfectly well that he's been sent by the Egyptian kingdom to oversee our endeavors. I've tried before and failed to convince him that we'll send word if ever there is need..."

Lady Bethy's eyes narrowed at the professor's words. As though he sensed her annoyance, Bathlolemew abandoned the masticated orange and fluttered to her shoulder. He rubbed the top of his head affectionately against his mistress's cheek – perhaps in an attempt to soothe her vexation. She reached up and returned the caress, stroking his feathered head.

"Well, no government will interfere with our little Verity, will they? We shall report him immediately. The authorities can't very well overlook such a base act of immorality!" Lady Bethy said staunchly.

Verity hoped that by giving Lady Bethy this excuse to rid herself of a man who had been a thorn in her side would beget forgiveness of Verity's supposed theft. She ached to mend the wound that she had torn asunder when she had invaded her friend's privacy and belongings.

Unable to decide whether it was best to bring forward that fateful subject at this juncture or to let sleeping dogs lie, Verity looked up into her friend's face. It was impossible to read, so Verity elected the latter course.

She then braced herself for what must inevitably come: The announcement of the death at the digging site.

Chapter Twenty-Nine

"Peace be upon you," called out the foreman as he entered the tent, dusting his feet off with a cloth twined around his fingers.

Removing the material that protected his face from the sun and dust, he continued, "I must deliver to you news that may give you both the utmost pain and joy. Dakarai has had an accident in one of the shafts in the night. I am afraid he is dead."

"How did this happen, Amr?" the professor inquired.

From his tone, Verity wondered if he was more concerned with his own culpability than for the loss of life of one of his workmen.

"It looks as if he was trying to investigate on his own last night – perhaps in seeking to receive a reward for his family, as you gave Kamuzu when he unearthed the headdress figurine."

With this last, he nodded at Lady Bethy. Verity well knew her friend's magnanimity and assumed that something had been paid to the worker who had disinterred the uraeus.

"As you know, several of the men have been caught trying to take away goods to sell to tourists on the mainland, but Dakarai is a good man. He has a small child and no woman to look after her. It is my belief that he would not otherwise have risked such dangerous work."

"Still – he should not have been down that shaft alone when he should have been sleeping. Let it be known amongst your men that no rewards will be given to those who do not have a witness to their discoveries – and in daylight. We've had enough trouble over trying to discover who stole our precious uraeus!"

Verity flushed with the memory of the little girl, but kept her peace, unwilling to draw attention to herself in front of so many.

Nodding once again, the foreman continued his report, "But in this death, some new life has been breathed into our excavations. We have exposed the remains of a child. It has not been buried as ceremoniously as others that have been reported in our sister camps across Egypt."

"A quick burial, perhaps," the professor mulled the words over in his mouth as though savoring a fine wine in the unattended confines of his own apartment. "Disease or... something else?"

"There *is* something else, Professor Easton."

The professor was far away in his own mind and soon

turned to rummage in his papers, muttering to himself.

"Something *else*, Professor!" called out Lady Bethy, impatient in her raised tones.

Bartholomew flapped his wings in tandem with Lady Bethy's stern words, but remained on her shoulder.

The professor did not respond until the bird repeated, "Something *else*, Professor!" in tones that mimicked his mistress's irritation.

"Oh, yes?" the professor was recalled from those long dead with which he was perhaps conversing in his mind.

"We have found what we believe to be the head of a sarcophagus, but we are unsure, as it is facing south instead of north."

"South? Why, this is almost unheard of. Why would it be facing south?! They are always buried facing north. Unless...unless it has been done purposefully. An act of revenge to prevent their peaceful crossover into the afterlife? Show me, Amr! Quickly, now!"

And the professor, absentmindedly placing his coat on first and his vest on second in his fervor, seemed to entirely forget that he possessed an ailing daughter and rushed out of the room without another word.

With a sigh, Verity fell back upon her pillows, and with that act, she fully relinquished her short-lived fantasy of ever possessing an affectionate parent.

Almost equally discomposed, Lady Bethy dismissed her servants and began to pace the room, her hands too shaky even to light one of her incessant cigarettes. Often, in the absence of Linette, she had requested that Verity assist her when she was in a trepidatious mood such as this. Glancing over to her in anticipation, she must have thought better of it after observing the pallid complexion of her friend.

Instead, she sat down in a chair on the opposite side of the tent and steadied her elbow on an ink-splattered writing desk until she managed to set one alight. Inhaling noisily, she studied Verity's features from afar.

Quelling under her gaze, Verity considered feigning sleep but thought better of it under the watch of Lady Bethy's keenly observant eye. Instead, without the weight of the professor's presence, she discarded her former resolve to remain silent on the issue that was so heavily felt between them.

Bartholomew, catching a cloud of smoke, sneezed almost the same moment that Verity began weakly, "Lady Bethy..."

"Hush, little dove. I know what you would say," was the unexpectedly kind answer.

"But I want to tell you..."

"No, I do not want to hear you say it. Your rooms have been searched thoroughly, and I think not only by my servants. I, myself, searched your person after you fainted, as much as it pained me to do so."

Verity could not help but feel injured that her truest friend in the world could think so little of her, despite the damning circumstances.

Pain must have registered upon Verity's features, for Lady

Bethy raised an arch brow and said defensively, “What could you expect from me, Verity Easton? It was *you* who trespassed on *my* generosity and trust. I simply paid it back in kind.”

The barbed words were spat out in such contrast to her former manner that, for a moment, Verity keenly felt the pain of them.

Shame did indeed weigh upon her heavily, but it was not guilt from the action that Lady Bethy’s assumptions thrust upon her.

“There was a girl,” Verity managed, at last, to faintly respond.

“A girl? What girl?” Lady Bethy snapped as she stamped out her cigarette on a pile of papers beside her.

Rather than listen for a response from Verity, Lady Bethy seemed distracted by the pile of letters that lay, helter-skelter, upon the professor’s desk. Suddenly, she took up the letter that she had so hastily ravished with her spent cigarette moments before. Concern, then anger, flashed in her eyes as she read it. However, the orange embers began to gain strength as they consumed more and more of the scrawled handwriting.

Verity gingerly continued, despite Lady Bethy’s abstraction: “I followed a girl. Through the camp. She led me to your tent. It was *she* who took the uraeus.”

At this point, the cigarette burn had all but ravaged the entire paper. As the charred burns crept toward Lady Bethy’s fingertips, she threw it upon the floor, stamping it out with her shapely boot. Verity had assumed it was a note of her father's making, but a small corner of the singed paper fluttered over to her and landed on her outstretched legs. Taking it in hand, the edges crumbled to ash, blackening her fingers. Examining it more closely, she noted that the writing was quite different from her father's – definitely a feminine hand with an inordinate amount of loops and underlines. Her eyes began to trace the letters of her own name...Verity. Singing her fingers, she stopped the cinders from intensifying so she could read the rest of it.

Unexpectedly, Lady Bethy began to laugh. Her chortling churned into a crescendo until tears streamed down her face. Verity's attention was drawn away from the paper toward her companion.

"Oh, to be young again!" Lady Bethy said at last, retrieving a compact from her handbag to ensure that her mascara remained intact. "To feel the discomfiture of a girl of your age rushing through my veins – ha ha!"

Using a minuscule dot of dusting powder to smooth out her features, she went on, "Now, Verity. You mustn't be ashamed. I know you felt some keen connection to the uraeus after having posed for the newspapers, but making up these silly stories simply won't do. I know you don't have it, so it must have been taken by quite another person. I'd bet half my fortune that it was that wicked Mr. Rashidi. But then, why would he hang about for so long if he was going to abscond with it to his precious royal officials that he's endlessly tedious about? Unless..."

Fixing her gaze intently on Verity, she urged, "Unless you saw something, little dove? Do not be afraid. I will not let that man intimidate you."

"No..." Verity said hesitatingly, confused by her friend's behavior, "In fact, when he came into my room, it sounded as though he was looking for it, as well."

"Was he, now?" Lady Bethy tapped her finger upon her chin musingly. "I thought that, perhaps, your prolonged illness could have been brought on by some poison or other, potentially administered by him to create a distraction for your father. Hmm...perhaps I was wrong."

Shrugging her shoulders, she continued, "Speaking of your illness, how are you feeling, my dear?"

Verity rounded the inquiry with another question, feeling more and more at ease now that she knew her friend did not believe that she had taken her prize: "How long have I been ill, Lady Bethy?"

"A few weeks," she said, "The Professor and I were quite prepared to send you to the mainland tomorrow if your condition did not improve. We had not done so before now, as we were afraid that moving you – especially by boat – could prove fatal."

Verity wrapped herself more closely in the blanket that had been laid across her, tucking it up under her chin. Wincing in pain, she looked at her hand. She had all but forgotten about the sliver from the knife's handle. Quickly, she hid it under the blanket, hoping Lady Bethy had not taken notice. Verity drew her knees toward her and stared closely at the little cross hatches that the woven material made. Shivering, the thought crossed her mind that it might have been better for her to have died while crossing the Nile rather than live to take the life of a man.

"Although you're still pale, little dove, you're looking better on the whole. We'll have you up and about in no time, I think."

Moving over to the bed, Lady Bethy pressed a tentative pair of lips upon the patient's forehead, leaving a smudge of lipstick between where the younger women's furrowed brows met. Simultaneously, Lady Bethy took the paper that Verity had subconsciously laid next to her while distracted by her friend's laughter. Half hoping to have read more of it, Verity allowed her friend to crumple the fragment without objection. Having lost the professor's shortlived attentions, she was loath to disturb this act of affection from Lady Bethy.

The woman gave the rumpled paper to her bird, who excitedly began to tear it to shreds with his hooked beak.

Sighing in surrender, Verity closed her eyes and allowed her friend to cover her with another blanket before she fell into a restful sleep.

Chapter Thirty

At first, the professor was unsure that they had, in fact, discovered Nefertiti at last. The sarcophagus in which she had been entombed was, indeed, elaborately painted with extraordinarily similar features to that of the famous bust by Thutmose. However, very little was found alongside her. There was no elaborate chamber filled with her favorite games, nor was there much jewelry or other priceless possessions. There were only three items they found beside her, buried beneath the sand: a headdress from which the sapphire-eyed snake had become detached, the mummified body of a lion cub with a single ruby placed in its mouth, and a scarab beetle statuette.

Shocked at such odd discoveries, the professor was perhaps even more puzzled by the lack of respect with which this revolutionary queen had been interred. Placed with her head pointing to the south, this meant that those who had completed the rituals for her did not believe her worthy of passing to the afterlife peacefully.

There were the traditional canopic jars containing her vital organs, fashioned after the four sons of Horus. As Nefertiti did not believe in any god but Aten, this seemed a strange addition to her supposed tomb.

Upon opening the lid of the sarcophagus, they also noted that the woman's mouth was open, as most mummies' mouths were, the ancient society believing that the soul could pass in and out of this orifice. However, with extended examinations, it was obvious that, at one point, the lips had been sewn shut. Someone, years later, perhaps, had pried open the lid and released the mouth from its stitchings.

This person or persons unknown had also tenderly placed more scarab beetles inside the sarcophagus at a much later date than the woman's original burial. In addition, they had carved into the inner portion of the lid several protective spells that could not have been originally engraved at the time of her burial.

These strange evidences led Professor Easton to believe that there might be an alternate chamber into which later carers of the tomb might have left more evidence that this mummy was, in truth, Nefertiti.

The search for this possible connected chamber, as well as the false door through which the dead were meant to pass in and out of in their travels to and from the underworld, was fervent. It was inconceivable that such a revered and powerful leader could have been buried without the necessities of the afterlife.

Then again, a great deal of mystery had always surrounded the ancient queen. Why had she been buried so far away from her husband and son? The red ochre fragments made up only a slender part of the riddle that begged to be untwined from the many tangled strands of history. Could Tutankhamun's displeasure at his mother's disruption of the old religion extend so far as to have her buried in such a doleful grave as this?

It was beyond belief...until the workmen began to hollow out more of the chamber. Mattocks in hand, their habitual singing returned as they continued in their pursuit into the very belly of the land of their ancestors.

Woven baskets were passed up on ropes, filled to the brim with ecru-colored rock and sand that crumbled as it was poured out – centuries of annual watery inundations having weakened it over time. Soon, they disinterred five more children of varying ages in addition to the one they'd identified before unearthing the adult woman's tomb. The professor initially believed this to confirm his original theory that they had all died from some ravaging disease, but upon further examination, ritual sacrifice was quickly determined to be the cause of these premature deaths. While most of the researchers felt the weight and sadness of this diagnosis, the news genuinely excited the professor, as records of Nefertiti documented that she had given birth to six daughters, aside from her son, Tutankhamun. As though in confirmation, each mummified child was identified as female.

This made the professor push the workers harder than ever before. The shaft they continued to dig extended deeper than any others they had attempted. One worker, overworked and exhausted, mistakenly began to burrow farther to the right than he had been instructed. At first, his companions were upset by his blunder, but, fortunately for him and the entire party, he quickly encountered an enormous tablet upon which a distinct inscription had been chiseled.

Down came the professor, hoisted upon a rope until his solid, leather-bound shoes touched the tip of the ladder – so deep had they delved that both mechanisms were necessary for his transport. He was led into the cavernous chamber until he came face to face with the information for which he had yeared.

By torchlight, he brushed away eagerly at the engravings, interpreting as he went. Symbols were known to be read in almost any direction, so it took some mighty guesswork on the part of the professor as he exposed the precious glyphs, but at last, he was able to make sense of them.

After scribbling his findings down in a little black notebook with a minuscule pen (both had been a gift from Verity upon his last birthday), he requested to be assisted back to the surface.

Verity waited in anticipation at the top of the shaft, having rushed there once she heard that the professor had been called down for the discovery. As his face came clear of the darkness and was illuminated by the sun, Verity's memories also resurfaced. She held her breath as she watched the professor's head emerge exactly as Dakarai's had done on that fateful night.

Momentarily slipping back into her entranced dream, she moved toward him, her hands clenching at the sides of her silken dress, her golden bangles jangling as she did so. The image of the lecherous man was before her once again, and she steeled herself in defense. She reached out her hands as though to push the man back.

However, as the professor began to speak, her glazed expression returned from that other world and fixed clearly upon his familiar face. Fists had formed from her hands, grasping his shirtsleeves. No bracelets cuffed her. No white, flowing material gathered at her waist – just her simple, usual khaki dress. Rather than shove the professor back into the chasm below, as her instinct prompted her, she instead attempted to lift him toward her. In her weakened state, she wasn't much help to the men who gathered on either side of them and hoisted the professor onto solid ground.

Triumphantly, with the look of a passionate zealot, the Professor hardly stopped to catch his breath before reading aloud from his little notebook: "I, Tutankhamun, he who placates the gods, Lord of the Two Lands, King of Upper and Lower Egypt, bury here my mother, Nefertiti. May her heart by Anubis be weighed and found wanting!"

A solemn silence fell upon the assemblage who had gathered expectantly as a euphoric rush of mingled terror and pleasure swept over Verity's heart alone.

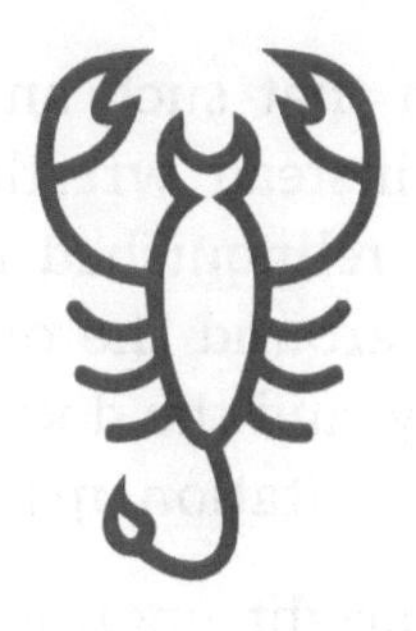

Chapter Thirty-One

All members of the encampment had been invited to view the grand procession of Nefertiti as she was removed from her tomb and transferred to a secure holding place, where it could be studied by other great minds alongside the professor. Her final resting place would there be determined, as well.

A sumptuous luncheon was to be served at the Old Cataract Hotel, and boats were arranged to transport all of the workers across the Nile and up to Aswan. The Egyptian Kingdom, delighted that their former queen had been at last identified, had spared no expense and made all the arrangements for the splendid event. It was rumored, that, due to Mr. Rashidi's connections, the king himself might even be present. However, preparations for it necessitated a pause in further excavations and investigations into the tomb and the writings on the great tablet.

Rather than allowing himself to be delighted by the

prestige and renown that such an event would afford him, the professor instead wrestled mightily against these decisions that relinquished his control over the discovery. Stamping around the open enclosure where he, Lady Bethy, Verity, and the doctor were gathered, he crumpled the official invitation up in his fist.

Verity was sitting upright upon a row of short, stone pillars. She distracted herself by studying the ethereal cerulean cloth that surrounded the enclosure as it billowed in the heightening breeze. It was rumored that the wind was the first indication that the annual flooding of Philae would soon begin. She watched the material intently as it swished this way and that, as though toying with the wind playfully. Wishing herself away from this antagonistic atmosphere, she longed to be back in her bed, resting and, perhaps, dreaming…

"Damn and blast it! It simply doesn't make sense. The waters will cover the entire operation before we know it. Everything will be lost. Besides, *I* found her. Nefertiti is *mine*! It should be up to *me* what happens to her."

Always possessive. Always placing himself at the forefront as though his was the only mind suffused with enough knowledge of the ancient Egyptians to have the privilege of unlocking their secrets.

Verity sighed resignedly and, as usual, meekly attempted to assuage his anger: "Professor, you must realize that this belongs to the people of Egypt as much as it does to us – in fact, more so. It is their queen and ancestor, after all."

"I realize no such thing – I make no concessions that she belongs to anybody but myself. If it wasn't for me, they would never have discovered her – not for hundreds of years!" was his impatient retort.

"I think you'll find that you are not alone in claiming the credit. You'd still be digging in that forsaken desert that even the Egyptian gods themselves wouldn't touch if it wasn't for *me*," interrupted Lady Bethy.

The peeress, too, had desired to keep the mummy nearby but could only leverage her importance enough to ensure that the professor could continue to study it during the off-season when Philae would find itself underwater and out of reach of fresh findings.

They would all have to resign themselves to the demands of the Kingdom of Egypt. Without the backing of the British Museum, the great Queen Nefertiti, although she garnered international laud, was entirely in Egyptian hands unless they, as so many before them, ignored the edicts and absconded with her body back to England. Mr. Rashidi's keen and watchful eye would never have allowed such an act. Although Lady Bethy had thrown her weight about enough to remove him from Philae, he had settled himself just across the river and kept a close eye on every boat that traveled to and from the island.

Despite the opposition of those who currently surrounded her, Verity was secretly glad that Nefertiti would remain in Egypt. She felt a pride in her mother's people – her own people. That they would dig their heels in and not allow another of their treasures to depart was a great comfort to her somehow. And although Mr. Rashidi's behavior, in general, had been inexcusable, particularly where Verity was concerned, she did secretly side with him on this issue.

The doctor, who had heretofore remained silent – although his eyes belied his surprise and disdain of the professor's tantrum – now cleared his throat and adjusted his spectacles.

"Shall we proceed with the examination? I believe I was called here to determine if Miss Easton is well enough to endure the crossing? I understand she desires to join the procession with the rest of you."

Lady Bethy and the professor nodded and moved toward Verity, along with the doctor. The triad of judges stood above her, surveying her closely as she sat before them with her hands folded meekly in her lap. Bartholomew turned his head to peer down at her from Lady Bethy's shoulder, and she had to stifle a laugh as he seemed to be sizing her up as much as the others were. As she endured their scrutiny, she straightened her dress and her back.

Endeavoring to look the picture of health, she had previously applied an inordinate amount of rouge to her cheeks and lips.

This deceit assuredly fooled the professor, as he commented, "Her complexion is much improved. Just look at that rosy blush on her face!"

His opinion delivered, he made as though to leave the airy enclosure to return to his work.

"Wait, Professor!" exclaimed the doctor, looking suspiciously at the false coloration. "I am not yet satisfied that she is well enough for the trip."

"What harm could a little boat ride do me?" Verity pleaded as she stood. "See? I'm not shaking or feeling faint one bit, and I've been able to walk, unaccompanied, to the edge of the enclosure and back!"

Verity stood and made a show of striding about the room, raising her knees high, like a soldier in a military parade, to demonstrate her regained vitality. As she trotted near Lady Bethy, Verity knew the makeup wouldn't deceive her as an authentically healthy complexion.

"Please," she mouthed to her friend, willing with all her soul for Lady Bethy to give her approval.

Allowing a grim, half-smile to escape her, Lady Bethy rolled her eyes and stated, "I suppose it would be cruel to not allow the child to attend the procession of Nefertiti to the mainland. After all, half her life has been spent with the professor in the pursuit of the discovery. Besides which, we *did* use her as our model in the newspapers. Her absence might, perhaps, be noted by the press. We don't want any more news of accidents and illness escaping after the nasty work they made of Dakarai's death. I'm excessively bored of all this talk of curses I hear among the men and read in the papers."

The macaw shrilly interpolated, "The curse! 'Tis the curse!"

They all stared at him for a moment, discomfited by his raucous disruption.

"The accident was unfortunate, indeed," said the professor unfeelingly. "It halted our progress of unearthing Nefertiti by several days."

"Unfortunate for his orphaned child, I'm sure you mean," said the good doctor stoutly.

The two men's spectacles glinted at each other in the sunlight as they sized each other up.

"Yes, for her as well," harrumphed the professor at last, turning on his heel and leaving the conversation, as well as the decision, to the others.

"So I may go?" Verity stood on the tips of her toes in anticipation of the answer.

"Yes, it seems that my would-be precautions have been outweighed by your father and your friend, but you take a care, Miss Easton. Until a short time ago, you were very unwell indeed."

"Take a care!" screamed the parrot, taking the opportunity of the breeze to soar in erratic circles above their heads.

"That will *do*, Bartholomew!" Lady Bethy said sternly to her pet, calling him back to her shoulder.

Ignoring the bird, Verity said firmly, "Thank you, doctor. I *will* be careful."

Without a backward glance, she exited the enclosure, luxuriously letting her hands run through the fluttering blue material as she passed it. So she would be part of the great procession of Nefertiti, after all. Looking up at the blue sky, she allowed the sunlight to rest upon her cheek and hugged herself in delight. She began to imagine herself floating across the Nile in regal attire, proudly presented to royal officials and grandly dressed ladies, finally feeling herself their equal as the professor's consequence was at last assured in the annals of history. Perhaps, if she played her cards right with Mr. Rashidi, she might even be presented to King Fuad and his wife. Queen Nazli Sabri was rumored to have one of the largest jewelery collections in the world. Verity had always longed to witness such displays of wealth and grandeur, and now, she finally had a hope of doing so.

Her fantasy came crashing down as she realized that, once again, she had nothing suitable to wear. There was no time to send away for a frock, nor did she believe that the professor would care to be bothered with such trivial requests at such a juncture.

A jolt of rage passed through her as quickly as a streak of lightning. She stopped abruptly, fingering the lioness brooch that she now always wore upon her person.

Just then, a black scorpion scuttled across her path, paused in its trajectory as it sensed her, and reared up, poised to strike. Usually, the sight of so deadly a creature would send her into a state of frozen rigidity with a strangled scream caught in her throat.

Instead, the wave of anger rushed through every limb until she lifted her foot and, careless of her safety, stamped upon the creature, grinding it into the earth with the heel of her shoe again and again until it convulsed in the aftershock of death.

Chapter Thirty-Two

On the day of the grand event, Verity began wandering through the encampment, testing her strength to assure herself that the trip would not be too much for her. She inhaled the sights and sounds that surrounded her. The men, commanded to tidy their work, were filled with as much excitement as she and seemed to make more of a show of moving tools, tarps, and the like, rather than truly accomplishing their mandated tasks.

Upon returning to her tent, Verity observed that a beautifully pleated chiffon gown, edged with golden silk, had been laid out upon her bed. Gasping in delight, she hastened to it, eager to inspect the charming fabric. Across the edge of the hem, there had been stitched intricate markings made up of familiar hieroglyphics that one of the workmen had taught her. There was a circle with a dot in the middle, an ankh, a scarab…

Gradually, she made out the full phrase and read it aloud:

"The very life of the manifestations of Ra, beloved of Waenra."

Why, this was the throne name of Nefertiti. Verity was overcome with pride as she fingered the ridges and grooves of the exquisite embroidery.

Assiduously sponging her dusty skin to perfect cleanliness, she felt a rush of nervous excitement as she drew the handsome garment over her head. As she did so, a paper fluttered to the floor. Verity caught it up. It was addressed to her, and she realized that it must have been tucked away in the folds of the frock.

After settling the garment onto her person satisfactorily, she installed herself at her dressing table to peruse the missive:

> *Little Dove,*
>
> *I know we've had our differences of late, but I hope you will accept this token of my forgiveness, a plea for yours, and a peace offering between us. Be sure that you ferret out that scarab bracelet (the gold should match perfectly), and I've made sure there's a little loop upon which to fasten your lioness friend that you say gives you so much courage.*
>
> *I've also taken the liberty of packing you a little bag, which you'll find under your pillow. These governmental affairs can be rather drawn out and dull, and I believe the feast isn't until long after nightfall, which leaves us many hours without food or drink, sadly. You'll find what you need in there when the time is right.*
>
> *Your faithful friend,*

B.

Gratitude filled Verity's soul for this staunch friend who, it seemed, would let nothing quell her stout heart. Obediently, she removed the lioness brooch from the simple khaki garment she had just thrown off, then ferreted out the scarab bracelet from amongst her belongings. Ceremoniously, she placed them on her midsection and wrist as though preparing for battle. Then, locating the aforementioned satchel from beneath her pillow, she made her way to the boat launch to meet her friend.

Dozens of men were gathered at the shores of the Nile. Verity vainly attempted to push her way through to where Lady Bethy and the Professor were to meet her. The workers were talking and laughing loudly, and Verity was swept up in the crowd, hardly able to move of her own accord.

A wave of excitement rippled over the assembly as they witnessed an elaborately painted boat, designed especially for the occasion, pull into the dock. Verity was meant to travel with her companions on that boat. Calling out for assistance, she tried to make her way toward it, but a surge of workers swarmed around her, making it impossible for her to walk in the direction she intended. Instead, she was unceremoniously knocked to the ground, her ankle twisting in a wrench of pain as someone stamped upon it, quite by accident.

The man looked down at her, but his eyes did not register sympathy, as she expected. In return, a white-hot rage overtook her heart as he moved away from her without another downward glance.

Just as she was about to suffer the same injury from another heavy tread, a familiar voice called out, "Miss Easton!"

Asim shouted at the men nearby, "Aibteaid! Move away!"

The crowd parted under the direction of the foreman, although none stopped to assist. Helping Verity to her unsteady feet, Asim wrapped his arm around her and removed her from further danger and the unthinking crowd. As he deposited her gently on top of a low barrel, she looked at the state of her new dress and moaned pitifully.

"My dress! Just look at the state of it! This tear can never be mended, and there's not a soap in the world that will remove that stain! Oh – will I never have just *one* frock that does not suffer a dreadful fate?"

"Your dress?" Asim laughed heartily, then grimly said, "It is the state of your *foot* that is of more concern, I think."

Looking down at her ankle, she could see that it was swelling up, a nasty red welt appearing where it had been trodden upon.

"I shall fetch the doctor now," Asim said reassuringly.

"No, no, the doctor is not here, Asim," Verity replied hastily, "He is not to be in Philae today. He has patients on the mainland and is not set to meet us until the banquet tonight."

"Very well. I shall accompany you to your quarters, then."

Verity shook her ebony locks energetically.

"No, I simply *must* get to the boat. The professor and Lady Bethy will be expecting me to join them. Besides, I can't be left here on my own. It wouldn't be safe…"

Verity's concerns were not, necessarily, for her own person, but for what she might do if left to herself while this frenzy of bitterness continued to wash over her. She felt ill as she thought back to the scorpion that had so nearly stung her only days before. If she could do that to an animal whilst awake, there was no telling what harm she could do to an innocent worker, left behind to guard the dig.

A loud shouting and singing commenced from the men, and Asim stood up on a crate to see what was causing the cacophony.

"It is too late, Miss Easton. Your boat has already departed."

Sighing in exasperation, she dusted off as much as she could of the dirt that besmirched her dress.

"You are welcome to join me and some of my men on another boat that has been prepared. There are many traveling over, but you will be safe in my company."

Nodding her assent, she accepted the arm Asim proffered to assist her. Standing up, she winced, but in her determination not to miss at least some of the eminent event, she limped bravely in the direction in which Asim attentively led her.

Settling into a place at the end of the barge, Verity bemoaned her colossal bad luck. This was no elegant boat commissioned by the Egyptian king to ferry the eminent discoverers of Nefertiti, but instead, some last-minute hire from a local fisherman. Verity was seated next to a net that reeked of the man's occupation, and she wished that she'd had the foresight to bring a perfumed kerchief to stifle some of the smell. A few medjed fish had been left tangled in the strands and trembled as though still alive as the boat shoved off the dock and began making its way across the mystic Nile.

Attempting to ameliorate her feelings in the admiration of the dazzling waters and the anticipation of the forthcoming celebration, Verity breathed the cooling air deeply into her lungs. She watched the sun as it began to sink below the horizon, creating a glittering reflection of sunset hues in the deep waters.

The momentary beauty and pleasure she found in the scene were cut short when she espied the rigid back, then the head, of a creature emerge from under the surface. The slits in its eyes seemed to examine her with almost evil intensity until it lazily lowered itself back into the depths.

A crocodile.

Verity had, of course, been warned of them and even seen them occasionally sunning themselves on the banks – at a safe and spacious distance, of course. But this one was so threateningly close to the shallow boat that her heart veritably beat itself into a frenzy until she could feel it pulsating heavily within her throat and around her ears.

She became almost lightheaded – the thrill of the encounter battling against the fear that never truly left her soul. Straining to catch another glimpse of the animal, her eyes began to water in the attempt as the river surrounding them lay perfectly still – the ripples of the boat the only movement that altered the glass-like surface.

Sitting back, she rubbed at her aching ankle, wondering what sad creature would become the bloodied feast for the crocodile. Suddenly, hunger gripped at Verity's own stomach with an undeniable pull. She realized that she'd had nothing to eat since her meager breakfast. Such had her excitement been that morning that her tasteless though sustaining gruel had been more than usually ashen in her mouth. However, now, after feeling the blood rush avidly through her veins, she felt absolutely ravenous.

Pulling with shaking fingers at the strings of her bag, she at last managed to open it. Contained within were a lovely loaf of brown bread, some fragrant cheese, and a small vial of wine. Verity rarely imbibed, mainly because the professor still believed her to be a child and forbade it expressly after hearing of her tipsiness at Lady Bethy's dinner. Lady Bethy, as was her usual custom, expressly ignored the professor's ban and often allowed Verity to partake in many piquant palliatives whenever he was not present.

Verity ate and drank ardently, soaking up the bitter wine that dribbled down her chin with a bit of bread to prevent further disaster to her frock. It felt so good to fill her belly. The hearty food steadied her, and her dizziness drifted away completely.

As she tore off another bite of the bread, her teeth fell upon something hard that tasted of metal. Puzzled, she drew the loaf back from her lips and studied it intently. Something blue and shining sparkled at her. Rife with curiosity, she pulled the bits of crumbling bread away from it.

Feeling an immense shock of recognition, she revealed the lost snake of Nefertiti's headdress.

Astounded, Verity stared at it as one entranced. Holding it limply in her hand, her mind passed beyond time or thought...

A man called out, drawing her back into immediate consciousness of her surroundings, and she glanced away from the artifact and toward the voice at her side. Quickly, she tucked the treasure away into her bosom, folding over the lapel of her dress to secure it carefully.

The voice had come from a man beside her. His face was shadowed, for he had inserted himself betwixt Verity and the dusky light of the sunset. He must have been completing some necessary task for the boat to maneuver successfully across the wide river. As he moved closer to Verity and out of darkened obscurity, recognition passed through her mind.

It was the man who had stamped so heedlessly upon her ankle near the docks on the island.

Without thought for her aching foot, or perhaps because of the pain that wrenched within it, she stood and, with all the momentum she could muster, toppled the man overboard into the watery depths.

He emerged for a moment, gasping for breath and help.

Watching with delight, Verity saw another form emerge

shortly thereafter, its mouth wide, its teeth long and sharp. Grasping the flailing arm of the man between its iron jaws, it dragged him down again, tumbling, splashing, drowning…in undulations of desperate hunger and extinction.

Chapter Thirty-Three

The boat rocked dangerously as several of its passengers, hearing the cry, rushed over to the side to witness the man's demise. Many pointed to the water just as the tips of his fingers disappeared below the surface. There were shouts and talk of trying to save the man, but all knew too well the power of a crocodile's deadly underwater dance. There was no hope of a rescue. All they could do was call out to each other to take a care as a few leaned over the side. Then, as the vessel steadied, a silence fell upon them all.

Asim's voice came floating toward her from the front of the boat in a hoarse prayer of supplication. Verity expected the others to join in, but it was Asim's voice alone that drifted out across the Nile, the rhythm of the boat's engine almost overpowering his unsteady tones.

Verity realized that she had been holding her breath and, at last, let the tightness in her chest release.

Could she really have gotten away with it?

None of the men looked at her with a scathing eye. Nor did they bind her hand and foot, as she would expect if they came face to face with a murderess.

Unsteadily assured of her external safety, she began to turn her eye inward.

What could have possessed her to do such a thing? Until now, she had excused her previous conduct over the matter of Dakarai's death with the severed rope. After all, she had been dreaming, and until now, she had supposed that sleepwalkers had no real control over their actions.

But this...this was quite a different situation. Intentionally, in a rage of revenge, she had taken the life of this man. True, he had done her harm and had neither offered help nor displayed the smallest hint of remorse, but did he deserve to die?

Verity pondered profoundly upon this transition from the meek, obedient girl she had always been to this vengeful woman with murder carved upon her heart. Perhaps living amongst civilizations made up of people long absent made her comfortable with the thought. She expected to feel regret, horror...but no emotion redolent of virtue came to her.

Instead, she felt eminently superior, satisfied that her actions had taken such a turn. Verity's internal compass had always pointed sharply toward duty and obedience. How had her life led her to this? Perhaps if she had possessed a loving mother, it was conceivable that her morality would not have taken such a lethal turn. Or perchance if the professor had not been quite so distant and preoccupied...

Verity shrugged her shoulders. It did not matter any longer what she yearned for. She felt liberated from the confines of society. Now, it was possible to take whatever she wanted – exacting revenge for the slightest insult, demanding retribution for those who dared to abuse her.

The boat moored abruptly, making Verity lunge forward with the impact. The snake ornament went flying from her bosom, knocking against the side of the boat and falling, hidden, under the wooden planks.

Blindly, she felt for it, her fingertips scratching desperately upon the floorboards. Panic gripped her. The men began to disembark, and she was terrified that they would see her with the uraeus, report it to Lady Bethy, and ruin their recently reforged relationship.

Ignoring the stench of the decaying fish and the splinters that waged war on her tender hands, she continued to search frantically. At last, her hand closed around the cold, twisted metal.

Straightening up, she surreptitiously placed the snake in her bag, glancing around to assure herself that the discovery was still hers alone. Moving toward the front of the boat, she alighted with ease. No one hindered her progress through the crowd, and she felt suddenly triumphant. Not a single man dared impede her now, and she no longer needed assistance with her injured ankle. It did not disturb her comfort.

As she walked away from the embankment, nearly all the workers' eyes were drawn toward her stately form. Admiration passed over several faces, despite the disheveled state of her dress, and many a man confessed to themselves that Miss Easton had indescribably become a veritable beauty overnight.

Just outside the banquet hall, Verity was arrested by the sight of two figures gesticulating wildly behind a large, overflowing bush of jasmine that was set against the wall in a ceramic pot. The jewels that bedecked the dress of one of the figures flashed in the flooding of light that poured out from the front of the building. Verity knew that a dress made up of such adornments must belong to Lady Bethy.

Nearing them, she could hear voices raised in alarming argument.

"I tell you, she belongs in Egypt! You shall *not* cart her away from the people who love and adore her – who have, for decades, searched for her remains! Take a few trinkets and baubles if you must. That should satisfy your vanity and the British Museum or wherever you choose to bestow them."

The voice was familiar – low and rich. It was assuredly Mr. Rashidi.

"Oh, my dear sir! We haven't even unearthed 'baubles'– as you call them – of any significance! And even if we had, do you think I'd let this priceless treasure slip through my fingers? I want my name down in history as the woman who financed the discovery of Queen Nefertiti! Nothing shall stop me from taking what is mine. Your gods certainly will it, or the fragment would never have come to me in the first place."

"My country thanks you for your contribution to this discovery, but it does not – *cannot* belong to you! You must see this. I have warned you from the beginning that you are trespassing upon things that should not be meddled with!"

A loud guffaw escaped the lips of Lady Bethy, "Surely you do not expect me to believe such claptrap as your curses and spells."

"I do not expect you to believe anything but that which you have set your heart upon, Lady Elizabeth."

"I will take what is mine. We both know I have the power to remove from you everything you hold dear," was her foreboding reply.

The man lit a cigarette and seemed, for a moment, to be quelled in this passionate dispute. The flame flickered in his face, the light dancing across his exasperated expression for a moment.

"I will tell you this," he continued, letting a puff of smoke escape his lips as he neared his opponent, the whisps lingering in her face until she waved them away with a defiant brush of the hand. "*You* will regret removing her from her people."

With a swift movement, he had hold of Lady Bethy's arm, his lit cigarette dropping searing ash onto her silken skin.

Crying out, Lady Bethy wrenched her arm away, knocked his cigarette to the ground, and spat back, "There was a time I believed you to be a gentleman, Mr. Rashidi. That time has long since passed, and I regret every moment in which I thought well of you."

"And at one time, I thought you were the most attractive woman I had ever seen. I even briefly entertained ideas of matrimony when we first met, but your greediness and disrespect of the traditions of my people belie your beauty."

Lady Bethy laughed, her voice echoing gratingly in the night air. "You men throw about your opinion of your attraction to women as though it was a badge of honor to be bestowed from on high."

Laughing even louder, she continued, "Your approval is neither a prize worth winning nor is taking your hand in marriage one I ever aspired to. You disgust me."

Lighting her own cigarette, she said, "As for your traditions...I know more about them than even you can hope to imagine. Did you not know that I am Egyptian myself?"

This last line was delivered in perfect Arabic. She lunged at him, the emblazoned tip of her own cigarette mere millimeters from his face. Flinching, he closed his eyes and turned his head, obviously expecting her to return his misdeed. Veering at the last moment, Lady Bethy merely squashed the embers of the cigarette upon the wall behind him. He recoiled as fragments of hot ash flecked his ear.

Silent, he looked her over calculatingly as she turned on her heel with supreme grace and moved away from him and into the well-lit building without a backward glance.

A fiery mania broke free within Verity's soul as she watched the scene unfold. This man, who dared to insult and threaten her kindest friend in the world, should not – would not – get away with it a second time. Verity recalled when he had bruised Lady Bethy's arm during the dinner where she had announced her intention to fund the professor's dig. If he could do so much in public, what other threats and abuses might have happened if they had ever met privately within the past months?

With resolute determination, Verity skirted the shadowed wall of the hotel so as not to draw the attention of Mr. Rashidi. Once inside, she determinedly marched into the dining hall. Scanning the busy scene of feasting guests briefly, she observed a spare seat. She sat down for a moment at the table, miming eating a bite or two of the food that was soon placed before her. Furtively, she grasped a fine-edged knife from her silverware and slipped it into her bag.

In a matter of minutes, she was outside again. As her eyes adjusted to the darkness, she surveyed the pots of flourishing jasmine where the altercation had taken place. Mr. Rashidi was there still, as she had hoped, sitting on a bench only steps away from where the ember of his cigarette still flickered on the stone pathway.

As Verity neared him, the scent of the blossoming jasmine flowers intoxicated her until her senses were overcome when mixed with the heat of the night and the vengeance in her soul.

Silently, she crept behind the tangled vines, her footfalls hushed as the clatter of voices and dishes echoed from the dinner. She was directly behind him now, electrified by the power she was about to hold over him. Her breath stirred the hair at the nape of his neck. Seizing that hair, she wrenched his head back and pressed the knife to his windpipe. The action felt familiar – as if she had done it before.

"Stop!"

Verity had half-expected him to plead for his life, but this voice was from quite another quarter. Looking up, she could see the figure of Lady Bethy before her.

Restraining herself for a moment, again, she heard the word as though it was the chime of a church bell, calling for her penitence: "Stop!"

Listening to the guidance of her friend, she took the knife away from Mr. Rashidi's throat and placed it between her teeth. With the agility of a panther, she used a few jutting stones of the wall behind her to hoist herself over it, then disappeared into the darkness.

Chapter Thirty-Four

Two young boys were throwing rocks at a thin vagrant in a shabby, yellowed dress at the end of an alleyway that was checkered with light from the linens that had been hung out to dry above. The young woman had been scavenging for food that was traditionally their quarry of a morning, and they were attempting to take back their right to it by what little means were available to them in their immediate vicinity.

Therefore, it was with bloodied lip and swollen eye that Verity made away with her miserable portion of breakfast – someone else's discarded dinner from the night before, no doubt. For days after her attack on Mr. Rashidi, she had purposefully starved herself, wallowing in hidden corners of the vast city of Aswan. Fearful of being recognized, she chose the simplicity of death from hunger over facing the realities of the unrecognizably bloodthirsty creature she had become.

When hunger truly gripped her, she had briefly

considered selling the precious possessions that remained in the bag that Lady Bethy had given to her. She soon threw away this idea in disgust – partly because she somehow couldn't bear the thought of parting with them and partly because she felt she deserved to meet the unceremonious doom of death as punishment for her wicked crimes.

It was only when the kindness of a strange woman, shrouded from head to foot in dark cloth, had extended a few fruits to her in passing that hope for life again returned to her veins. Soon after, she had discovered the remnants of the meal for which she paid so heavily with her cuts and bruises now.

Bending low over her hard-won food, she found herself face-to-face with a golden-eyed alley cat. It held a bird between its teeth and tore the flesh from it with relish. Verity imitated her feline companion, feeling so ravenous that she felt no shame in her eagerness. After their mutual meals were complete, the two of them cleaned themselves thoroughly: one with its rough tongue - the other with her fragile evening dress.

When strength returned to her limbs, Verity began to ponder her next actions. She could not bear to return to Lady Bethy or the professor. How could she, after having committed two murders and attempting a third? Verity began to worry that she could even be responsible for more.

What about the violent death of poor Linette, who had pierced Verity's leg with a needle and was sentenced to strangulation for the pains she took to help her? Or Lady Bethy's former husband, the lecherous Mr. Larcher, who had been discovered with his throat slit? Verity fretted within herself as she recalled the familiar feeling that came back to her when she had placed the knife at Mr. Rashidi's throat.

The only explanation was that Verity was suffering under some sort of divergent fugue state during which she had almost no control and, in the past, could not even fully recall.

Haunted by these thoughts, she followed the cat out of the alleyway and through several near-empty streets until she reached a small outcropping of palm trees. Men were hard at work here, shimmying up the rough trunks and using hatchets to hack away at the fronds. They threw them down to their comrades, who, in turn, bound them up in neat piles, placing them inside rough-hewn, two-wheeled carts.

Verity knew they would be taken away to be fastened onto humble rooftops, used as firewood, or even deftly fashioned into furniture. Forgetting her troubles momentarily, she admired the agility of the workers as they leaped up, up, up…

A loud rattling disturbed her ears as it drew close to her. At last, withdrawing her gaze from the expert workmen, she turned to see a motorcycle bellow its way from the street and onto the dirt path upon which she had been wandering.

"I say!" called out the man as he removed his goggles and gloves. "Hullo, there! Do you know where I might find some petrol?"

Most of the men did not even look away from their work.

Verity guessed that many of them did not speak English, as they were not used to dealing with foreigners in their line of work.

Obstructed in his desire, the man turned off the engine and dismounted. He was walking toward the group of industrious workers when Verity caught his eye.

Addressing her, he said, “Do a fellow a favor and tell me where I might buy some gasoline.”

Shrinking inside of herself, she startlingly recognized the voice and mannerisms of none other than Captain Bardot.

She felt his eyes upon her and half-turned away from him, but it was too late to escape. He caught her hand in his, and she felt forced to face him. Concern, then recognition, washed over his features.

“Miss Easton? Is that – could it be you?”

He pulled her toward him, his other hand outstretched in solicitation, but she fended him off with her palms.

“No, no, you mustn't touch me,” her dry lips cracked as they parted, and her voice, which she had not much use for in the past days, was raspy and feeble.

Captain Bardot withdrew a pace as though to intimate that he would obey her commands, but his voice belied his concern for her: “Are you well, Miss Verity? Has something happened to your father?”

Shaking her head, Verity hid behind her unkempt hair as it fell into her face.

“I assure you, I am quite well, Captain. Although I am

surprised that you recognized me after all these years."

"You probably don't recall, Miss Verity, but I did catch a glimpse of you at Lady Elizabeth's dinner party many months ago. I have been traveling throughout Egypt for some time, and she invited me when our paths happened to cross. It was I who helped you out of the boat when you trip..." his eyes shifted back and forth as though searching for a less insulting term, "...disembarked."

Verity recalled the flash of a captain's uniform that had caught her eye as she had nearly fallen from the barge that evening.

"I hardly recognized you then," Captain Bardot continued, "It was not until much later – after the sad tragedy of Lady Elizabeth's maid – that I heard your name mentioned and put two and two together."

The captain inexplicably blushed at this juncture. "But when I recalled our first meeting, it was your eyes that I remembered, Miss Verity. I've never forgotten them, as their coloring is absolutely unique. I've not seen the like before nor since."

At this point, he searched the very eyes he spoke of as she looked up from the ground, where she had been studying a beetle cross between them, a laborious stream of sand pushed this way and that in its wake. Recovering himself after this strangely intimate compliment, Captain Bardot swept his arm suddenly toward his motorcycle.

"Can I give you a lift somewhere? I assure you, although it's loud, it is quite safe."

Again, Verity shook her head, then thought better of it.

There *was* a private stream which she used to wash her hands and face occasionally, but it was a long way to walk, and she'd not had enough breakfast to sustain any such journey on foot.

"Why, yes, Captain. I do think you could take me somewhere. I'm…I'm due to meet a friend for a swim. I'd lost my way and met with some pleasant children who lured me into a rather energetic game, which is why you find me in my present state."

She let a mirthless laugh escape her, endeavoring to purport herself as the picture of casual unconcern.

"You look as if you've met with a few ruffians rather than playing a game with children," the captain returned skeptically as he looked more closely at the state of her apparel. "Are you sure I shouldn't be dropping you at a police station or something of that sort?"

Verity, longing for safety and understanding, almost told him all of her woes then and there. Unconsciously, she placed a hand upon the bag that was slung across her shoulder. As she felt the bulky outline of her treasured ornaments, she drew an incomprehensible feeling of comfort and strength from them.

Again, the hollow chuckle echoed through Verity's dry throat, "No, no, Captain. I'll be clean soon enough after my swim. I didn't want to wear anything too refined for my adventures, so I just grabbed this old rag from the bottom of a drawer somewhere, and I didn't even bother with my coiffure."

Tousling her hair, she relaxed her shoulders and moved toward the motorcycle with confident strides.

"It's a fine piece of machinery," she cooed. "I can't wait to see how she goes. Shall I get on before or after you?"

The man must have been convinced by these mild flirtations, for he placed her on the bike. It started with a loud, satisfying growl and hummed along pleasantly as Captain Bardot followed the directions she shouted in his ear. After a while, they arrived at the riverbed that emptied into a pleasantly deep and clear pool.

Admiring the glistening, beryl-blue waters, Captain Bardot seemed to turn half a mind toward having a swim himself, but Verity deftly fended him off.

"Shall I stay until your friend comes?" he queried entreatingly, an eye on the inviting waters.

"Oh, no – he'll be along any moment, I'm sure," was the swift reply.

He started, then recovered himself. As Verity unentwined her arms from around his waist and alighted from the contraption, he looked her up and down calculatingly from the corner of his eye, evidently considering that he might have misjudged her sense of morality.

She tried not to acknowledge his look and allowed a haughty expression to pass over her features, as though male companions for such intimate activities were an everyday occurrence for which she was not ashamed. Verity did not know where the lie had come from – but her vague idea that he would be more apt to leave her alone if he thought he might have a jealous lover to contend with seemed to have worked.

Revving the throttle a few times before taking off, he

suddenly cut the engine. Verity, worried that he had, after all, changed his mind and decided to defend her honor in the absence of the professor, cast him an exasperated look.

He caught the glance but said abashedly, "I'd nearly forgotten. I met the most remarkable woman when last I stopped over in England. When I mentioned I was returning here to check up on the progress of a friend's excavation (I had read the news of Nefertiti, you understand), she mentioned that she knew you. She said that she had sent you an extremely important letter recently, but, as she had heard no reply, she entrusted a missive to me to pass along. I have it here, somewhere."

Feeling around in the inner pockets of his leather bomber jacket, he drew out a crumpled envelope and handed it to her.

"Strangest thing," he continued, "Said she knew my mother. I don't quite know how – Mother's been dead these twenty years, and this woman didn't seem anywhere near old enough to have met her. Said Mother was proud of me becoming a captain so young..."

Emotion took over the man's countenance momentarily, but he recovered quickly. Puzzled, Verity held out her hand for the letter, thanking him as he turned it over to her.

She watched him thoughtfully as he drove away, his engine sputtering as it was perhaps now dangerously close to running out of petrol. Silently sending a wish into the universe that he would not return on foot after driving it to the brink of emptiness, Verity placed the letter safely under a dry rock and began to bathe.

For although she expected no companion, she did wish to clear her body and mind momentarily. Lost in the waters that were comfortably warmed by the sun, she reveled as the dust and dirt washed away from her. Closing her eyes, she began a waking dream.

Chapter Thirty-Five

The dream began much like the others. She was walking within the open corridors of a palace, clothed in a bathing robe of exquisite gossamer. Inspecting her wrist, she noted the scarab-bedecked wristlet – a token of immortality and the cyclical nature of life. Glancing down, she perceived the ruby lioness – a symbol of war and triumph. Touching her forehead, she traced the shape of the serpent – the protector of pharaohs long before she ever dreamed of ruling alongside her husband.

Torches blazed, flickering in upon the water of her private bathing pool as the scimitar moon cut through the star-studded night sky.

Slipping out of these accouterments, she placed them tenderly on the side of the pool before descending into it. The water was warm and bubbling gently – the effect of an underground spring around which she had built the temple to Aten. Reveling in the sensuality of the waves created by her very presence, she leaned back until the mellow din of the palace faded into muted melodies as the water washed over her ears.

A shadow passed over her body. She opened her eyelids lazily, wondering if a servant would dare disturb her at such an hour, but she could make out no figure in her surroundings. Relaxing once again, she slipped her head below the water, holding her breath for a moment.

Just as she was about to resurface, she felt hands placed upon both of her shoulders. Perplexed at who would commit such an offense against her person without permission, she tried to raise herself above the surface to demand an explanation.

The interloper held firm. She struggled. Still, the iron clasp of the two hands was unyielding. Her lungs began to burn. She was desperate to resurface. Fighting, clawing, then finally screaming, she felt the water wash down her throat.

Verity came to consciousness with a gasp. The water was indeed filling her mouth. She coughed, choked, and made her way to shore, where she vomited violently upon the hot and clinging sand. When she was at last able to catch her breath, she looked around to discover her attacker.

Not a soul was in sight.

It had all been a dream – the water in her lungs pouring in from her own foolish drift into a half-waking hallucination.

Shivering somehow despite the oppressive heat of the sun that beat down upon her, she dragged herself over to the flat, smooth rocks nearby.

As her hand passed over one such rock, it knocked away her makeshift paperweight and revealed the letter that Captain Bardot had passed on to her.

After a few shaky but deep intakes of breath, she struggled to open and remove the paper from its pasted environs. A newspaper clipping fell from where it had inadvertently stuck to the back of the letter. It was an article from a British newspaper, announcing the disinterment of Nefertiti. Verity, curiosity burning deeper than the fire in her throat, opened the letter and read the vaguely familiar, looping and heavily underlined writing:

My Dearest Miss Verity Easton,

I'm not certain you'll remember me. We met on a train and then again in a market oh – is it almost ten years ago now? I can't hardly believe it – so much has happened since then. To me, not to you. Well, to you, too, I suppose. Why, you must be quite the young lady, all grown up and flourishing in that divine Egyptian sun.

I did enjoy Egypt. I've been meaning to return there, but I have been so engrossed with my work here, you understand. So many souls needing my help, and I'm very happy to give it to them, but you see, they can be such a nuisance when one wants to travel.

I do apologize for the tea stains – it's that Pimsy cat again - she simply hasn't got any manners when it comes to letters of the utmost importance. She's gone and upset my cup without the slightest hint of an apology.

I'd hoped to hear from you after my last letter, especially since I didn't think you were the type of girl to leave these things long – you took such great care of your father, didn't you? So you can see that I felt I must write another to you, just to be sure the other didn't go astray.

Do be terribly, terribly careful and take good care of yourself and be sure to not let anyone get the better of you – most especially yourself.

Oh! I've quite forgotten to put in what I meant to tell you – and that is you are the reincarnation of Queen Nefertiti. I'm a medium, you know, and when I purchased the bracelet for you, it was at the behest of the goddess Isis. I had met with her to obtain some special healing balm, but she followed me around that market for a bit – rather annoyingly, I thought at the time – as I needed to find another crystal for my practice, you understand.

When we discovered you eyeing the bracelet, she was most insistent that it belonged to you in your past life. I did not think it of much consequence at the time, but she did mention, in passing, your past murderous tendencies. She said the bracelet needed to come to you and for your former self to return for some special ceremony or other? Perhaps, if your memories have returned, you'll understand what she meant.

To be truthful, my attention was rather distracted by her husband, Osiris, who is a most attractive god and who had just arrived to recall her to their bedchamber. It made me quite blush the things he said to her. I don't blame her for hunting for all the pieces of his magnificent body and putting them back together after he was murdered by that naughty brother of his. I certainly would have done the same to reclaim him.

So as I mentioned, do be careful now that your father has discovered Nefertiti's tomb. You might feel closer than ever before to your past life, and I felt the need to warn you.

Yours ever,

Vamelda Anstruthers
Medium of the Occult

Chapter Thirty-Six

Already feeble from lack of food, a brush with death, blood on her hands, and more, Verity became dizzy with the knowledge this missive held. For it was absolute truth – of that she was certain – despite the willowy and bewildering way in which it was presented.

Everything fell into place. Her heritage, the bracelet, her homicidal intentions. This woman, long-dead, had been reawakened within her, taking over her already shy and relenting personality until soon there would be nothing left of Verity.

Nefertiti. The woman who would kill over the slightest inconvenience or displeasure. The seductive queen who made a pharoh desire her. The strength of a monarch who possessed the conviction that revolutionized a centuries-old religion. The assurance of a magnificent regent that would lay claim to Egypt as her own when her husband, Akhenaten passed over to the underworld.

Verity was no match for her. She had felt her creeping gradually into her veins, possessing her more and more as she collected the trinkets that must have belonged to her.

One thing pricked at the back of her mind. The bracelet coming into her possession by way of this medium was understandable. Even the discovery of the uraeus was feasible due to the professor's work. But how had Lady Bethy come to acquire the lioness, and why had she gifted it to Verity? Above all, how did the snake come to be baked into that loaf of bread?

After all the woman's generosity and their close friendship over the years, Verity could not countenance that Lady Bethy had any foreknowledge of this ancient, previous life.

Curiously, Verity emptied the contents of her bag onto the scorching slab of rock. With a tentative fingertip, she pushed each of the elements around until something caught her attention. A wing of the scarab had loosened and was hanging a few degrees away from the other. Fascinated, she knelt before it in a prayer-like pose. Anyone observing her would think she was offering supplication to the ancient gods.

Gently, she pried apart the wings of the lustrously colored beetle, spreading the jade to either side until it revealed a strange, concave shape – as though something else belonged there. Turning the other two trinkets over in her hand, she perceived that the back of the lioness's head was the perfect shape. Hands shaking, she locked the lioness into place. As she did so, the ruby slipped down from between the teeth of the lion, and another hollow opening appeared.

A firey flood of rapture filled her, and she felt the power of this other self pressing her, urging her to further action. Nearly blind with scintillation, she felt for the undulating shape of the serpent and slid it between the teeth of the lioness until it locked into place. As she did so, the clasps of the bracelet unfolded, revealing length upon length of linked metal until it extended enough to form a necklace.

Verity knew what it would mean if she bound the metalwork around her neck. She would disappear, and Nefertiti would overtake her completely.

Her timid soul had often longed for the strength and power of the men and women who surrounded her. Lady Bethy, for instance – if only Verity had her command, her confidence, she could do as she liked and to hell with the rest of the world.

But she also knew it would mean giving over all of her pure morals and kind heart to Nefertiti's iniquitous soul. Slowly, she raised herself from the ground, holding the fate-binding amulet in her open palm. Could she…should she dare?

A voice came from behind her: "Do it," the tone was breathy and low, full of tremblingly fervent emotion. "Go on – place it around your neck. You've come this far."

Hesitatingly, Verity turned around. The individual she saw was so entirely unexpected that she lost her breath for a moment.

"Go on," Lady Bethy continued. "It is time to embrace your destiny."

Although the sun shone brightly in her eyes as she looked up at her friend, Verity could make out three men behind Lady Bethy, leering at her menacingly.

Hardly able to tear her gaze away from them, she felt compelled to study the necklace again.

“Why do you hesitate? Is it some schoolgirl semblance of shame? Bah! You are too far gone to think that Verity can save you now. Put it on.”

Verity saw one of the three men halfway draw a curved dagger from its sheath that was attached to the cloth wound around his waist.

Vacillating between the two lives she had to choose from, she clung to the one she knew best.

Trembling, she pleaded, “Just let me be myself – my own self – a little while longer, Lady Bethy. For our friendship's sake? For the professor's?”

The older woman tipped her head back as she laughed maliciously.

“Friendship? Do you think I've kept in touch with you all these years for your charming personality?”

Verity bit her lip at the harsh words.

Again, a nefarious chuckle fell from Lady Bethy's lips, “There were times when I could hardly stand the utter banality of your company. But I knew it would all pay off.”

“Then why?” tears filled Verity's eyes as the betrayal of the only tenderness she had ever known began to crumble away as the tips of the peaked sand dunes against the wind.

"For one, your father's interest in discovering Nefertiti. For that alone, I would have befriended you. But it was the bracelet that made me realize the one I've sought for all these years was before me, as innocent and gullible as a little dove."

Hearing the formerly tender appellation spoken with such antipathy made Verity's heart sink to the depths of her soul.

"You know, then. You know everything. You know I'm…"

Verity was about to say, "a murderer," but Lady Bethy interpolated, "Queen Nefertiti."

"Yes," she continued, "I knew about the necklace. In fact, I believed you had already put the pieces together when you threatened Mr. Rashidi days ago. Your weak and meek little soul couldn't possibly do something that audacious. I believed Nefertiti to have already taken you over then."

"But why? Why, Lady Bethy?" Verity pleaded, tears spilling from her eyes in abject anguish.

"Put on the necklace, and you will assuredly find out," Lady Bethy replied, narrowing her eyes as she drew closer to her prey.

The other two men drew their weapons threateningly, pointing them toward her as they flanked their mistress.

Bowing her head in defeat, Verity raised the jeweled band to her neck. Hungrily, Lady Bethy and the men watched her as she did so. As Verity pressed the metal against her skin, she heard the familiar roar of a motorcycle.

Chapter Thirty-Seven

As the clasps twined behind her neck, Nefertiti instantaneously sensed the danger that surrounded her. One of the men resheathed his saber and unfastened a length of rope that was looped at his side. As he closed in on her, she held out her hands as though humbly accepting the binds that he began to coil around her wrists.

When he started to tie and tighten them, she twisted her arm and wrenched the rope toward her, forcing him off balance. In the same motion, she pivoted on her toes and whipped the rope until it arced in the sky. Almost in a dance, she wielded her makeshift weapon as a snare and enclosed the man's neck. Behind him now, she pulled back with all her strength until she could see the skin at the back of his head turn an ugly purple hue. Gasping, he crumbled to the ground.

As she turned to face the other guards, she found that one was already on the ground, apparently unconscious. The other was doing battle with Captain Bardot. With a well-placed jab, the valiant captain disarmed his opponent, and the sword went flying toward Lady Bethy's feet. The peeress screamed and lifted her legs in a sort of jig to avoid it lacerating her ankles. The ever-present Bartholomew moved from her shoulder to the top of her head, pulling at her red locks in an attempt to steady himself.

Another rigorous punch from the captain and the third man fell backward, sprawling on the ground, apparently insensible as well.

Nefertiti began sprinting toward Captain Bardot as quickly as she could, moving only out of her trajectory when she espied Lady Bethy collect the discarded saber.

Holding it awkwardly, she took a wide swing at Nefertiti as she passed. It managed to slice a tear in her bedraggled dress, but blade did not encounter flesh.

An outcry of disappointment escaped Lady Bethy's throat as Nefertiti grabbed the stunned Captain Bardot by his wool-lined collar and steered him toward the motorcycle.

Lady Bethy called to her bird, who had at last disentangled himself from her now-wild coiffure, "The eyes, Bartholomew! Go for the eyes!"

The couple mounted the bike while the macaw flapped around their heads, attempting to obey his mistress's commands. Nefertiti protected them both with waving arms and received only a few scratches as Captain Bardot turned the engine over and sped down the dirt road, kicking a cloud of sand up in their wake.

Nefertiti held fast to her defender, feeling a rush of pleasure at the quick pace of the motorbike that made the palm trees move past them in blurs of brown and green. She had longed for control of this body – longed for the freedom that complete dominion would offer her. Verity's spirit was all but gone now. She was a mere shadow tucked away in the corner of this youthful form.

Wrapping her arms more tightly around the body of this man, she pressed her chest against his back. He removed his hand from the throttle to caress both of hers for just a moment. Soon, he turned off their dirt pathway onto a main road that led back to the city.

Pulling up to a humble inn of sorts, he cut the engine and helped her off her seat with an outstretched arm.

"Come with me, Miss Easton. You'll be safe here."

Nefertiti searched her body's memories, allowing Verity's knowledge to resurface momentarily.

"No!" she said decisively. "They'll find us here. A simple inquiry as to your name will place us in their grasp much too quickly. We must move on to another place and use a name that is not our own."

Surprise registered on his features, but he nodded and disappeared under the covered awning which led into the hotel.

Returning a quarter of an hour later with a suitcase, he set to work strapping it on the back of the motorcycle. Nefertiti had not wasted the time in which he'd left her alone. Speaking with some wide-eyed children nearby, she had received the information she'd sought with little trouble.

"Where to?" said Captain Bardot as he brought the engine to purring life once again.

Ensuring no one was near enough to hear, Nefertiti gave the direction in his ear. Acknowledging with a slight inclination of the head, they were soon bumping along the road southward.

They traveled for some time, winding along the glittering Nile, and Nefertiti again feasted upon her newborn senses. This alone she shared with her host body's soul: the almost worshipful affection for her Egyptian homeland and all the beauties it possessed.

The sand that burned in her lungs did not bother her. She was breathing in the earth of her kingdom, and the very fact that she could taste it in her mouth meant that the life that stretched before her was full of possibility. The dips in the road transformed into rushes of heady excitement. It was merely her own Egypt fighting back against the progress of humankind, as it had always done. She reveled in the battle and knew that she would come forth triumphant, as she'd done in the past – building up monuments, temples, and cities...using its own rich resources to overrule it.

Captain Bardot shifted in his seat, leaning back against her in an act of assurance. Now that she, the great Queen Nefertiti, had returned, she could use this man to forward her ambitions – to recover and rest as she plotted her next move.

Heretofore, Verity had taken a modicum of strength from Nefertiti's emerging soul and used it to take revenge on the people who offended her. Soon, she would remedy this misplaced and feeble attempt to control those who stumbled, unthinking, across her path.

Nefertiti's first rule of commanding power was not death, but seduction. When that failed or was impossible, yes, a throat slit here or a commanded execution there was certainly in order. With Verity's timid and unassuming temperament, she'd had no hope of exercising any charms of the flesh. But there had always been in her but the sliver of petulance upon which Nefertiti had been able to prey – a biting bitterness toward the way the world treated her. With that, she could draw herself upward within Verity's being, lending her the tenacity to accomplish the vengeance that lived already in her heart.

Without the amulet's endowments, Nefertiti had little control over the motivations of her actions, but she did glory in the moments when she had been able to assume command of Verity's body. Slitting Mr. Larcher's throat had been particularly satisfying, as any man's unwelcome advances she had always considered punishable by death. So clever of her to use the letter opener that was a staple of each of the hotel's amenities.

Linette had also deserved her fate – how dare a servant so carelessly harm this sacred vessel that served to bring her, the great Nefertiti, back from the dead?

As Captain Bardot slowed the motorcycle, she was drawn away from these thoughts to the immediate present. They had arrived at a village on the banks of the great river. After weaving through several side streets, Captain Bardot pointed inquiringly at a sign perched precariously above a lodging house. Nefertiti gave him a squeeze of assent. He turned the next corner and parked the motorbike in an alleyway behind some stock that seemed to be working as impromptu storage for a nearby bazaar. Appropriating a tarp, he covered the motorcycle so that only the very tips of the wheels were left to be seen. He tugged a few boxes and barrels into place around it until it resembled nothing more than another heap of the surrounding excess inventory.

"That will do for now," said the captain decisively. "She's such a looker, so we'll need to hide her more convincingly and safely than that, soon."

Nefertiti looked it over appraisingly, made a few adjustments to the tarp, and nodded her approval.

Taking her by the hand, the gallant captain pulled Nefertiti along beside him.

As they rounded the corner and entered the lodging house, he said in a low, intimate voice, "You'll have to excuse me, Miss Easton, but we'll need to pretend that we're married. I hope you don't mind."

In response, she stood up on her toes and brushed his rough cheek with her lips. A semblance of a smile made a few lines crinkle at his temples.

"Mr. and Mrs. Jones," he announced to the lodging house matron, money outstretched on his palm. "We're here on our honeymoon."

Nefertiti lifted her head to the ceiling and laughed gloriously and uproariously in this extraordinary twist of fate.

Chapter Thirty-Eight

Nefertiti stretched her long, supple limbs across the clean, white sheets. The proprietor of the lodging house kept the room very tidy and changed out the linens every few days. Nefertiti would have insisted on every day but knew that she must bide her time before all the demands she deserved could be met.

It had been remarkably simple to coax the captain into her bed. After all, they were already forced to share it, and it didn't take long before he understood that the look in her alluring eyes was giving him permission to possess her.

They were natural together, like the pushing and pulling of the tides – their true identities hidden from the rest of the world. She allowed him to call her Verity. His given name he had told her during the first time they made love, but she had quickly forgotten it, not caring for him with any genuine rushes of affection. Thus far, she had gotten away with her carelessness by ascribing to him the tender epithets lovers often use for one another.

Nefertiti had probed him that first night – demanded an explanation as to why Lady Bethy had been able to uncover her whereabouts. He had, as Nefertiti had guessed, met with Lady Bethy quite by accident when seeking the professor. Not quite believing Verity's story, he had sought the her father's whereabouts. This led him to the Old Cataract Hotel, where he had encountered his hostess from the dinner she had invited him to so many months ago. Distressed and eager to find Professor Easton, the truth spilled out of him.

In return, Lady Bethy had informed him that Verity had been missing for some time and called together several servants, promising to return with the young lady in tow. Captain Bardot only took enough time to ferret out and inform Professor Easton, then returned to the pool, at his behest, to ensure his daughter's safe recovery. Astonished to find that Lady Bethy and her guards had more nefarious motivations in mind than a reclamation, he jumped into instinctual action to save her.

Nefertiti rewarded his blind faith amply with both praise and the pleasures of the flesh. Such loyalty would serve him well in the future Egypt she intended to build once she claimed the throne that was rightfully hers.

For her people would reembrace their queen when they discovered who she truly was – of that, she held no doubt. She would need to garner support from those who held power and sway. Captain Bardot was a wealth of information as to the nature of the current king's reign. Already once divorced and with rumors swirling that the present royal couple got along not at all well, Nefertiti was assured that she could soon convince and seduce King Fuad into marrying her.

There would, of course, be a grand unveiling of her true identity, then, soon after, a reclamation of the reign of the pharaohs. It would not be long until the entire magnificent country would return to the sole worship of Aten.

Nefertiti raised herself to her knees and held up her hands in supplication for the great god to assist her in this, her monumental but predestined task. If that meant genocide or enslavement, well then, she thought, with a shrug of her smooth shoulder, so be it.

Leaning over the bed, she lit a stalk of incense in prayer. As she did so, the sacred necklace she never removed shifted, and a piece of metal at the clasp snapped. For a moment, her vision blurred, and she felt a little faint. Strange…her reincarnation should mean that she felt no pain or fragility.

She raised herself from the bed as the captain entered the room. He'd been collecting their breakfast from their lodging house keeper. He presented it to her on a wooden tray. As she reached for a rice-stuffed grape leaf, the necklace slipped just a little from her neck, most of the chains still clinging to her skin.

Looking up into the face of the captain, she felt a rush of affection. Shyly, she met his intense gaze of desire. Leaning down, he kissed her on her crimson lips as a rosy blush flushed her soft cheek. The lapse to tender emotion lasted only as long as their attempt at lovemaking. Verity felt shy and retreating as he caressed her. Without the fiery heat of Nefertiti's nature, it was quick, passionless, and incomplete.

When the captain stopped, Verity withdrew to the edge of the bed, gathered her knees to her chest, and began to cry a little. The necklace was hanging at full tilt now, about to slide completely from her neck. Verity knew that she faced a fateful choice: Keep this man's obsession with her alive by securing the necklace or remove it and risk losing him forever. Trembling, she reached her hand up and...

She actually loved him. This fool of a girl was still in there, albeit small and insignificant, and she was falling for this captain – this nobody. True, he was useful to her now, but soon, Nefertiti planned to discard him for larger prey. Ensuring that the clasp could not fail again, Nefertiti stood up and began wrapping herself in her robe.

"You bore me," she said suddenly to her companion.

"What? I –" he broke off as she turned to him with the blazing look that made him covet her so.

"We need a change of scenery," she said flatly. "You will take me to Philae."

He, too, stood and started to dress himself.

"But what of Lady Elizabeth? What if she's waiting for you there?"

He was obviously reluctant, especially since her commanding self-assurance had returned. Moving over to her, he began tracing her waist with his fingers and licked his lips in anticipation of a kiss. She pushed him away with a look of revulsion in her eyes. Verity's feelings of naive devotion toward him repulsed Nefertiti. She was in no mood to encourage his lust now.

With her usual haughty toss of the hair, she stated matter-of-factly: “It is flooded this time of year. No one will be looking for us there.”

“But why, then? Why do you need to return there, especially if it’s flooded? What good would that do?”

Within her, Nefertiti knew that she needed to say a prayer where her body had been laid to rest – to say goodbye to her former mortal form and to gather strength from Aten for the great task that lay before her.

“Arrange a boat! I did not request that you comprehend the tasks I lay before you. I merely require your obedience!”

“Obedience?” he said with a look of perturbation. “Why would you think…?”

Pain and confusion transformed his handsome features as she landed a heavy slap across his face. Almost instantly, her lips were upon his, and their bodies melted together for a moment.

As they pulled apart, he pushed again for more, but she turned from him.

“You may have what you desire once you have secured our passage to Philae. It is not much to ask, is it?”

“No…” he said, watching her intently as she began to dress. “No, it isn’t.”

After completing his own ensemble, he left promptly to accomplish her demands.

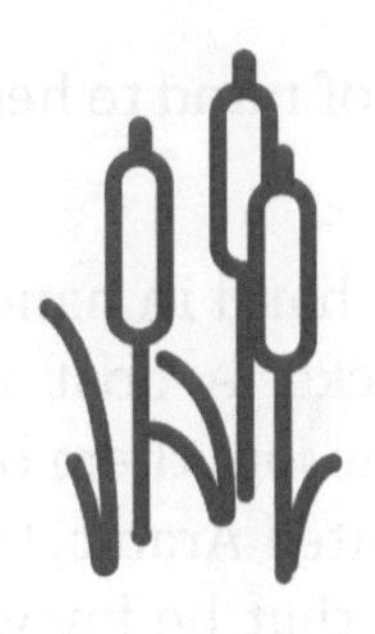

Chapter Thirty-Nine

As they slipped out in the heady evening air, Nefertiti admired the way the colors of the sunset melded into those of the desert. It was as though it was one continuous canvas of pinks and oranges, splashed together by an amateur artist's hand, with no brushstroke that distinguished the earth from the sky.

Walking quickly, Nefertiti kept her face hidden with a light scarf. Her clothes, obtained by the captain weeks before, were plain and unassuming. He had wanted to lavish upon her marvelous and rich fabrics, but she had called him a fool, knowing that in their current plight, they would not wish to draw attention to themselves.

There would be time aplenty for extravagance once she was reinstated as queen. Now was the time for blending in as much as possible. The captain, too, was dressed in the robes of a local tradesman for which he had bartered earlier that afternoon in pursuit of hiring a boat. At least he'd had the presence of mind to heed her counsel in that regard.

They made their way, hand in hand, through the village and down to the docks. A boat was at the ready, its owner insistent that he join them on their journey. After the captain, in his limited Arabic, tried to ameliorate the man with assurances that he knew what he was about, Nefertiti soon tired of the argument. As she stepped into the boat with a firm foot of assurance, he attempted to block her pathway. Annoyed, she pressed forward, but she was no match for the experienced boatman.

"Very well. You may come with us, but we will not pay you the full amount if you do," she said in their native tongue.

He gesticulated madly, calling them thieves and liars.

"We will pay what is owed to you when we reach our destination," she capitulated in exasperation.

"Where is this destination?" he demanded.

She gave him the direction, and although his eyebrows raised in surprise, he nodded and began making preparations to depart.

Once they had shoved off from the shore and were well out of sight of any lookers on, she whispered to the captain to hand her his foldable knife. He responded with a quizzical look, but her self-assurance always cowed him into submission to her every whim.

Tucking it beneath her robes and within her bosom, she knew what she must do to protect them both.

Night had almost wholly swallowed day by the time the island of Philae was in sight. Wordlessly, she stole next to the boatman and thrust the knife into his side until he toppled into the bottom of the boat.

Apparently not realizing what Nefertiti had done, Captain Bardot leaped to the man's assistance.

"Is he having some sort of fit?" exclaimed he as he tried supporting the man's head.

Soon, a pool of blood, shining in the reflection of the city lights that echoed from the shore, became visible to him. Cooly, Nefertiti lit a lantern and held it to the man's face to assure herself that he was, in fact, dead.

"What on earth? But how?" he queried, looking up at her in shock.

Her complete lack of mortification, or even interest, was plain upon her features, and Captain Bardot's eyes widened.

"Why?" he demanded, watching her wipe the bloody knife on the folds of her robe.

"Did you not see the little girl to whom he signaled as we left the dock?" she responded calmly.

"No, I –"

She interrupted, "I recognized her instantly. They are undoubtedly spies for Lady Elizabeth."

"But how could you know?" he inquired as he closed the man's eyelids in an act of acceptance and finality.

Nefertiti did not respond, but she spoke the truth. The girl had grown, but it was indisputably the same little imp who had led Verity to the uraeus in Lady Bethy's quarters. At the signal from their boatman, she had made off toward a nearby telegraph office that sat on the shores of the river, and Nefertiti knew that their plan would soon be thwarted by her enemy.

This did not deter her from her task, however. They would merely need to exercise more caution in their pursuit.

"This is too far, Verity. Too far!" exclaimed the captain suddenly. "You don't know that he was a spy for Lady Elizabeth. Where is your proof? I will have no more to do with this. I will not accompany you further if this is where your tendencies lie."

"You cannot think that I would do so lightly?" she demanded. "He could have done far worse to us had I not acted quickly."

"I will take us to shore. This man must be returned to his family. We must say it was some sort of accident."

He began to steer the boat away from the island and toward the eastern embankment.

"Very well," Nefertiti said in an emotionless voice.

Privately, she resolved that it was time to be rid of this man. She could always blame the death of the boatman on him if officials became involved. Meekly, she would attend him to the shore, then take the boat along to Philae without him.

Unable to find a suitable dock that would be private enough to not draw attention to their indelicate cargo,

Captain Bardot pulled onto a patch of bare sand flanked by reeds. Under cover of the darkness, he gathered the bloodied body in his arms and made to deposit it upon the shore.

As he disappeared beyond Nefertiti's sight, she began to shove the boat back into the black water, wading out up to her knees as she pushed with all the force of her being. She was arrested in her undertaking as unknown hands were laid upon her. One calloused palm covered her mouth while three others gripped either of her arms, dragging her back from the river.

Chapter Forty

"To the brig!" screeched the eminently recognizable voice of Bartholomew.

Although Verity could not make out his bright feathers in the moonless night, she could see that he, as usual, haunted the shoulder of Lady Bethy. Before she could make any sort of protest, the men dragged her toward the sound of the bird who continued his raucous chant. Soft, nimble fingers undid the clasp about her neck, and the amulet was removed from her breast.

A great weight was lifted from Verity's soul. She thought of calling out to the gallant captain for help, but the hands that covered her mouth would have stifled any such cry.

Flanked on either side by the men and led by Lady Bethy, the intimidating troupe made their way through a copse of palm trees that seemed to follow along the banks of the mighty Nile. Halting at a boat, one of the men took her none-too-gently by the arm and forced her onto a seat within it.

Without wearing the trinkets, Verity felt almost wholly in possession of herself and her faculties. She had no desire to exert herself toward an escape. After a brief ride, she noted tall, ominous trees that seemed to emerge from the water before them. As they neared, she discerned that they were not trees at all but towering columns that stretched to the sky as though in supplication to the gods above them.

They had arrived at Philae.

The oars disappeared silently as they cut into the river. As they passed through a double colonnade, the boat was suddenly pitched to the side as one of the men unintentionally struck the stone of a pillar. Verity reached out on either side of her to steady herself.

Flames licked the surface of the obsidian-colored water, and Verity could begin to make out her surroundings by the light of many fire torches rather than the lanterns that were in usual use at the encampment.

As they passed on, Verity took in her surroundings. Many familiar sights were almost unrecognizable as the boat floated several feet above what was usually dry ground. The flooding had fully taken hold of the temple, the Nile drowning from the melting snow of the far-distant Ethiopian mountains.

Verity strained to orient herself. In the flickering light, she could barely distinguish the tip of an upturned nose on either side of her. They belonged to two granite lions, which the professor had identified as the ancient protectors of the temple. The rest of their bodies wholly submerged in the water, their sightless eyes glinted eerily under the ripples as the boat and its passengers drew near.

Deep into the temple they navigated, taking turn after turn until Verity was dizzy in her struggle to retain some semblance of a pathway.

Brilliant viridian and coral markings appeared above a lintel under which they passed closely. She studied them as intimately as she could. A jackal-headed Anubis, kneeling before a scale in which a feather was placed on one side, a human heart on the other. Verity knew that it was this god who was believed to have determined whether or not an individual could pass to the underworld safely.

The goddess Ma'at, represented by the ostrich feather, was the epitome of truth and justice. If an person was found wanting, then the demoness Ammit, depicted laying hungrily to the side and with the head and gaping jaws of a crocodile, would devour them.

During their journey, Lady Bethy had been haughtily looking forward, as bold and unabashedly as a nautical figurehead carved into the prow of a ship. When they passed under the lintel, she turned back toward Verity, smiling at her with wicked triumph.

Soon, the boat slowed, and Lady Bethy alighted atop a dais, her skirt catching a bit of water as she ascended the steps of it to a stone throne that stood at the top. As elegantly as a queen, she sat in it, wringing out her dress in annoyance but still managing to make such a prosaic act look graceful somehow. The macaw fluttered to the back of the throne, following his mistress's actions with a curious eye.

Without a word, the two men unceremoniously dumped Verity out onto a slab of hewn rock, tossing the necklace beside her. It clattered against the stone and struck a canopic jar, which rocked dangerously for a moment, then settled back in its place.

The men removed the boat from the rock and propelled themselves back to join Lady Bethy. They took their place upon the dais, standing as sentinels on either side of her.

Curled up as small as she could make herself upon the raw, cold stone, Verity shivered uncontrollably. For although it was indeed chilly in the dusky shadows of the night, her soul felt far colder as she could sense that the life she knew was drawing to a close.

Chapter Forty-One

Lady Bethy stared at her expectantly from across the water.

"Well? Put it on, then," she demanded impatiently.

Bewildered, Verity gazed around her, but she could not see much in the darkness that seemed to swallow up the walls that surrounded them like a gaping beast.

As though reading her mind, Lady Bethy gave the slightest flick of her wrist, and the two men beside her each took a torch and set alight what seemed to be a creeping river of fire within the clay gutters that lined the upper walls of their enclosure.

For the first time, Verity noticed a dusky pile of material laid out beside her. Studying it more closely in the newborn light, she realized in horror that it was the remains of a mummified corpse.

"It can't be," Verity exclaimed.

"But it is," Lady Bethy shot back.

"Then you?"

"Yes."

"But how?"

"We replaced it just before the banquet, before it was even secured in the boat. Your father and his comrades are currently puzzling over a much different one."

"Whose?"

"Mine!" Lady Bethy ended their usual, near-preternatural melding of minds with a wicked glint in her eye. "I have no need of my old body any longer. I have been fully transformed, much as you will be very soon."

She clasped her bejeweled staff tightly, waving it back and forth admiringly in the firelight.

"Yes, this is my own amulet. With it, I am reborn, much as you are, though I have no permanent need of it now."

"I don't understand," said Verity tremulously.

Laughter rang out amongst the columns.

"Do you not, child? Do you not realize it even now, after having worn the necklace?" Lady Bethy licked her lips before slowly stating: "I'm going…to kill you."

"Kill me?" Verity's voice was high and thin as breathtaking bewilderment stuck in her throat.

"Why, yes, little dove. You must be sacrificed. That's the only way, don't you see?"

"Sacrifice? But I thought..."

"What? What did you think, foolish girl? That we were going to resurrect you for nothing?"

"But why give me the elements for the necklace? Why fund the dig? Why bring me back only to destroy me?"

"To prevent you from harming anyone ever again. To put a stop to your wicked plans. If we didn't do it, some idiot like your father would have, leaving Egypt open to your crazed religion and murderous demands. I always knew we'd have to bring you back to do it properly."

Tears ran down Verity's cheeks, blurring her vision.

Lady Bethy continued, hardly drawing breath as the truth spilled out of her, "We did not complete the rituals with which to seal your soul when your son and I buried you the first time. His heart was still imprudently softened by filial attachment, and thus you were laid to rest with the ability to be reincarnated."

"I will not be making that mistake a second time," Lady Bethy had suddenly transitioned into Egyptian.

Verity struggled to interpret but at last returned in the same tongue, "My...son?"

"You still do not remember? Place the necklace upon your throat, and you will," Lady Bethy's teeth gritted menacingly.

Obediently, with a great, heavy sigh, Verity did so, slowly clasping together the links of the fastener.

As soon as she closed the last clasp of the metal teeth, a

thrill – a rush of joy and heat and warmth returned to her. She placed a hand upon the petrified remains of her former self and lowered her mouth above the open one of the mummy as though ingurgitating every ounce of its essence. Raising up to her full height in a triumphant posture, a brazenly bewitching and reborn Nefertiti stood before her immortal enemy.

"You think that you can defeat me, Ankhesenpaaten? You have had many names since Verity has known you, but that is the genuine one, is it not? Oh, yes, I recognize you now. You were always jealous of my beauty and my power. Tell me – were you ever able to charm your way into the bed of that foolish son of mine?"

"Yes," Ankhesenpaaten responded casually. "And I convinced him to erase all but your name from every carving, every inscription that I could discover. Even your ridiculous religious reform was shattered as easily as glass upon stone."

"And yet, Egypt now worships a single god, albeit they know him by a different name," retorted Nefertiti.

"Many names or one name, it is not the god in whose name you murder, but for your own selfish pleasures."

"Pleasure was ever my goal, yes, but it was those who crossed me in my mighty work who felt the true wrath of Aten."

Ankhesenpaaten's laugh radiated from her, the sound leaping back and forth amongst the flooded hallways.

"You always claimed that the slaughtering of those who opposed you was the will of your god, but it was your vanity that could not brook a single offense."

Unable to form a retort, Nefertiti instead stated boldly: "I call upon the might of Aten, the only true god, to empower and protect me."

"The only protection you will find is from the elements, when we rebury your body in a shaft so endless, no professor will ever be able to discover it."

Nefertiti laughed with pernicious glee.

"That can never be," she said, deliciously wrapping her arms about herself in an exuberant embrace. "Now that I have a new body, you can be assured that it shall not be wasted."

"Is somebody there?" an echo of a male voice called out in an American twang.

Both women fell silent, suspended from their centuries-long battle momentarily by the modern sound of a propellor boat that began to rattle closer and closer to them. They must have taken a wrong turning somewhere, for the sound died away again.

Expelling their breath in unison, the two women stared with pure hatred at one another.

"Enough of this," Ankhesenpaaten broke the suspenseful stillness. "It is time for you to make your appearance before Osiris, keeper of the underworld! Kneel before the gods who sit in judgment upon you, Nefertiti!"

Inexplicably, Nefertiti felt a little of Verity's soul as it sought to escape. The sound of Captain Bardot's voice had returned to her heart the hope it had abandoned when she entered the temple. Struggling to overtake the other soul within her, she succeeded only in bringing the body they shared to its knees.

Satisfied but surprised, Ankhesenpaaten smiled at the development.

"Your heart has been weighed, Nefertiti. You have been found wanting!" Ankhesenpaaten withdrew an ankh and a flail from either side of her stone throne and crossed them ceremoniously upon her chest.

Momentarily entranced by the reverence-inducing act of the woman, Nefertiti's eye was drawn away by movement in the waters that surrounded her. Terror struck at her mind when she discerned that not only one, but three crocodiles slowly began to circle the altar, which was elevated a mere foot above the jet-black pool. Surreptitiously, she removed the knife from where it had been tucked away in her bosom.

"Ankhesenpaaten! Hear me!" called out Nefertiti, who had returned in full and commanding force. "You will never defeat me! You are led away by false goddesses and gods who demand what of you? To kill also? How does this make you any more worthy when the time comes for your heart to be laid on your so-called scales of Anubis?"

Mocking her in tone and tenor, she continued, "Who is to say that Ammit will not devour your flesh instead of mine? Did you not murder me in our past lives? Did you not hold me under the water until I gasped my last breath? Do you not intend to kill me now? I verily believe the blood that drips from your culpable hands will tip the scales out of favor of your ludicrous gods."

Stepping forward in her fervor, salient teeth snapped at her ankles, causing her to quickly return to the center of the altar. For the first time, Verity felt dread surface within this other soul.

“Ah, yes. You may not believe in Ammit, but you still retain your fear of her children! Is it not so?”

Glee erupted over the features of Ankhesenpaaten as one of the crocodiles began to climb onto the stone table as Nefertiti backed away, alarm awakening upon her countenance in turn.

“Your crimes were born of vanity, mine of justice. I only killed you then to stop your reign of horror and sacrilege. Your foolish son might have followed in your footsteps and allowed your new religion to overtake all of Egypt had I not saved him! One day, I shall return this great kingdom to her former glory, and all will bow to the gods they unwisely deserted long ago!”

Quelled momentarily but eager to defend, Nefertiti continued in a marginally depleted voice, “Egypt was becoming more wealthy by the day when I ruled her! What do you make of the blessings of your gods when my sagacity brought us greater prosperity than our people have ever known?”

“Sagacity, you call it? I call it greed! You were merely hungry for lucre – you took what you wanted and damned those around you to live in despair! You were insatiable and would have continued to ruin all who followed you had I not culled your esurience! And now, those crocodiles are about to satisfy theirs!”

Another crocodile emerged from the water and mounted the altar from the other side.

Without warning, all of the creatures retreated and vanished under the water. At first confused by their withdrawal, the sputtering of the motorized boat at last sounded within Nefertiti's ears, along with a voice that brought a bolt of joy to Verity's battered soul.

"Verity? Verity! Are you here?"

It was the stalwart voice of Captain Bardot again.

"She cannot be here," echoed another in calm, practical tones. "She would have had to take another boat."

"What do you call that, Mr. Rashidi?" Captain Bardot retorted triumphantly.

Verity's heart began to pound within her, stronger with each line delivered, even though she knew that it fell upon hostile ears as well as her own.

"I do not believe Verity would be so foolish," yet another voice chimed in with the other two, and Verity recognized it as the professor's.

As the newcomers drew near, Ankhesenpaaten's followers each drew a weapon from the confines of their belted robes.

"Kill them," she said easily, calmly, as though the lives of the three brave men were equal to a few gnats, swatted away in annoyance under the heat of the sun.

Chapter Forty-Two

As the boat drew closer, Verity's natural soul wrestled to resurface. She could see the outline of her love – her Captain Bardot. The exceptionally unyielding will of the Egyptian queen forced her back down, burying her deep within the body they shared.

"Verity, Lady Elizabeth, what is going on here?" demanded Mr. Rashidi, ever calm with his commanding presence.

"No two persons of such names are here present," responded Ankhesenpaaten with equal placidity.

"What is it? What are they talking about?" chimed in the professor, pushing his glasses up his sweat-laden nose as he blinked innocently around him. "Verity! What are you doing here, of all places? I've been terribly concerned about your safety. Come at once – I want my dinner."

Seemingly unconcerned or perhaps, unaware of the danger of the situation, he motioned for her impatiently.

He barely glanced at the two menacing men who were quickly moving through the water toward them – one wading waist-high, holding a cutlass aloft with both hands, the other beginning to swim with a dagger between his teeth.

As they neared the boat, the first man received a powerful kick in the face from Captain Bardot for his trouble, dropping his weapon upon impact. The other attempted to climb into the boat, but Mr. Rashidi firmly stamped upon his fingers until the man called out in pain, the dagger falling from his mouth with the outcry.

The boat began wobbling dangerously from the violence, and the professor was thrown back. His head was knocked against some ballast, rendering him unconscious. Verity cried out, worried that the professor was seriously injured, and Nefertiti was temporarily knocked from her internal throne with the momentary rush of filial emotion.

It was short-lived, however. Nefertiti soon took hold again, gleefully looking onto the fray as both of Ankhesenpaaten's men resurfaced and again ventured to board her rescuers' boat. As Captain Bardot leaned over, he managed to collar his quarry, submerging the man again by force. The other man was able to dodge Mr. Rashidi's quickest jabs and clamored into the boat, toppling over his opponent as he did so.

Mr. Rashidi, scrambling to his feet, gained the upper hand and placed the other man in a stronghold. Soon after, with one Herculean sweep of his arms, Captain Bardot drew his challenger out of the water and pinned the man's hands behind his back.

The two women looked on, eager for the conclusion of the scene to play out. One with the hope that she could fool these men into liberating her, the other, at a farther distance, straining to see the strength of her warriors.

When Ankhesenpaaten's men were secured in the prow of the boat and the professor, although still unconscious, was propped up as comfortably as his companions could manage, Nefertiti's fiery eyes turned upon her nemesis.

"You see? There is no hope for you, Ankhesenpaaten. Soon, I shall be free of you."

Her rescuers neared Nefertiti, the boat navigating between the dais and the altar. As Captain Bardot reached for the young woman, Ankhesenpaaten sighed dramatically.

"I was hoping it wouldn't come to such modern conveniences as this, but, under the circumstances..."

She nonchalantly withdrew a revolver from her sleeve and fired a shot into the air. All eyes turned upon her.

A shriek escaped her lips as a mass of red, blue, and yellow feathers fluttered to the ground around her. Bartholomew's lifeless body thudded beside her.

Taking advantage of Ankhesenpaaten's momentary distraction, Nefertiti lightly crossed over the boat and onto the dais in two swift bounds. With a strangled, threatening shriek, she leaped onto the throne like a hungry jaguar and straddled her mortal enemy. The knife she had previously removed from her bosom was clasped in her fingers, hovering inches above Ankhesenpaaten's breast. As she raised her hands to defend herself, the gun was flung into and swallowed up by the rippling water.

Nefertiti raised the knife to strike, but just then, the professor called out, "Verity? Verity, what on earth...?"

Those words recalled Verity to her own self. She turned to see the trio of men. Her father, confused and shaking, Mr. Rashidi, surprised but ever calm, and, at last, the captain she so desperately loved.

The look of adoration and concern that crossed his features decided Verity once and for all. His heart did not belong to her – it would never be so. Anger and jealousy raged stormily within her.

Bending over her prey, she gently whispered in Lady Bethy's ear, "Promise me you will end this, once and for all."

The eyes between the two friends met, one with mingled curiosity and terror, the other with finality and determination.

The knife plunged deeply into the heart of Nefertiti. Again and again, Verity managed to strike until blood pooled thickly upon the cloth of her dress. The body of Verity Easton fell to the side of the throne, the last spark of her soul draining from her face. The fierce and turbulent expression of the mighty queen melted away forever, leaving none but the softened and triumphant visage of the meek and loyal Verity in its place, fear and peace comingling strangely upon her delicate features.

AL-NIHAYA

Afterword

Thank you so much for taking this journey with Verity! If you've loved unearthing the mysteries of Egypt alongside her, please share your experience by leaving a review. Positive reviews mean the world to authors. I can't wait to hear your thoughts!

If you enjoyed the character of Vamelda Anstruthers, she also makes a more lengthy appearance in my first novel, **Hattie Vavaseur**. You can find it on Amazon, Audible, Kindle, Nook, and Barnes & Noble!

M. Rebecca Wildsmith

Made in United States
Troutdale, OR
10/17/2024